The Bri[...]

When proposal planner Riley is asked to plan a pretend engagement for an Italian billionaire, she doesn't expect to step in as his fake fiancée, too! But accepting Antonio's "proposal" sets in motion events that will not only change Riley's life, but also those of her mother and her best friend...

In Susan Meier's latest trilogy, get swept away to Italy with the bride-to-be as she accidentally falls for her pretend groom. Oops! Meanwhile, the mother of the bride takes on the father of the groom and gets so much more than she bargained for. And the bridesmaid goes head-to-head (and lip to lip!) with the best man!

It's all happening in The Bridal Party!

Read the bride's story

It Started with a Proposal

Available now!

And look out for the mother of the bride's and the bridesmaid's stories

Mother of the Bride's Second Chance
A Kiss with the Best Man

Coming soon!

Dear Reader,

Oh, my goodness!

These two characters took me on quite a journey. They were strangers who entered into an agreement to pretend to be engaged—for a good cause—who ended up being thrown together constantly. Usually against their will. Until suddenly they woke up and realized they belonged together...

Or did they?

They lived on different continents. They had different lives. She'd never found love. He was divorced. People used her. Everybody loved him. Her father had died. His dad was his best friend. She hadn't had a family. His family was close and loving.

How could they possibly be the right match? Especially since his marriage had been so bad and his divorce so ugly that he'd vowed never to marry again—and she wanted that. She wanted commitment and kids, the whole nine yards.

There was no way they could be together—or was there?

This is a fun, emotional story with lots of surprises and a few good laughs. I think you're going to love it as much as I loved writing it.

Susan Meier

It Started with a Proposal

Susan Meier

———

HARLEQUIN

Romance

Recycling programs
for this product may
not exist in your area.

ISBN-13: 978-1-335-59662-8

It Started with a Proposal

Copyright © 2024 by Linda Susan Meier

For questions and comments about the quality of this book, please contact us at CustomerService@Harlequin.com.

TM and ® are trademarks of Harlequin Enterprises ULC.

Harlequin Enterprises ULC
22 Adelaide St. West, 41st Floor
Toronto, Ontario M5H 4E3, Canada
www.Harlequin.com

Printed in U.S.A.

A onetime legal secretary and director of a charitable foundation, **Susan Meier** found her bliss when she became a full-time novelist for Harlequin. She's visited ski lodges and candy factories for "research" and works in her pajamas. But the real joy of her job is creating stories about women for women. With over eighty published novels, she's tackled issues like infertility, losing a child and becoming widowed and worked through them with her characters.

Books by Susan Meier

Harlequin Romance

A Billion-Dollar Family

Tuscan Summer with the Billionaire
The Billionaire's Island Reunion
The Single Dad's Italian Invitation

Scandal at the Palace

His Majesty's Forbidden Fling
Off-Limits to the Rebel Prince
Claiming His Convenient Princess

Reunited Under the Mistletoe
One-Night Baby to Christmas Proposal
Fling with the Reclusive Billionaire

Visit the Author Profile page
at Harlequin.com for more titles.

CHAPTER ONE

ANTONIO SALVAGGIO SAT in his favorite Manhattan restaurant with his favorite date, June Bronson, a petite blonde with a bubbly personality. Nights with June were always upbeat, positive, sexy. Every time he was in New York to see the family conglomerate's lawyer, he called her.

So why was he staring at the tall brunette hovering in the corner of the Tuscan style restaurant? Her hair had been pulled back in a bun at her nape. Her conservative beige skirt and matching sleeveless sweater made her blend into the mural of a vineyard on the wall behind her.

Though it was Sunday, she was also working. She had to be. Her focus and concentration were on a table in the middle of the room. Others might not have noticed that all the seating had been moved at least six inches away from that center table, but Antonio came to Sabato every time he was in the city. He saw the discreet distance.

A young woman with a violin appeared out of nowhere, stopped by the center table and began playing something soft and romantic. The guy seated with a woman who was clearly his girlfriend pulled a ring box out of his jacket pocket, rose from his chair and got down on one knee.

Ah. That was why all the tables had been moved a few inches away from that center table. The guy dressed in a black suit was proposing.

The restaurant fell silent. Waiters stopped pepper mills midturn. Forks stopped midbite. The hostess bringing in a pair of new diners came to a quick halt, putting out her arm to stop the couple following her. The air in the room shimmered with something intangible, something special.

The guy said, "Will you marry me?"

His partner's eyes widened before she blinked back tears. "Yes!" She jumped out of her seat. "Yes!"

He caught her in his arms to kiss her when he probably should have been sliding the ring on her finger. The brunette in the beige skirt hustled over. She took the ring box from his hand, extracted the ring and gave it to him, along with a significant look.

He jerked back from the kiss and put the ring on his new fiancée's finger.

Then, to everybody's surprise, a choir dressed in judge's robes danced in from the kitchen singing the alleluia chorus. After a second of silence, a burst of laughter filled the room.

"She's a judge," the future groom explained to the crowd, grinning as if he'd just won the lottery.

Another round of laughter erupted followed by a round of applause.

"She seems awfully young to be a judge."

Antonio murmured, "Hmmm," in response to June's comment, but his eyes were on the woman in beige. She'd obviously planned the proposal, gathered the chorus, hired the violinist. She'd noticed the groom's little faux pas of not immediately putting the ring on his girlfriend's finger. That was probably the choir's cue to enter. So, she'd hurried over and kept the proposal on track. Then she'd gone back to her spot in the corner, blending into the Tuscan-themed mural on the wall, as she studied the happy couple who accepted congratulations from diners near their table.

Antonio watched them too. He should have shuddered in revulsion—marriage was an outdated institution as far as he was concerned. A messy divorce had cemented that idea for him. Yet he couldn't stop thinking about that proposal. Low-key enough to be romantic and sincere—but with a spark of interest with the alleluia-singing judges—it was exactly what his grandmother wanted from him.

"Antonio?"

He faced June again. "Sorry."

She batted her eyelashes. "That was very romantic."

He snorted—but sadness tightened his chest. His grandmother had breast cancer and she was dragging her feet about scheduling her treatments. She'd been depressed since Antonio's grandfather died six months ago. It was difficult to get her to do anything. But scheduling those treatments wasn't just "anything." If she didn't pull herself together and start treatment, her depression would end up making her cancer, and therefore the treatments, worse.

An itchy sensation raced along his skin. Every argument he or his father had made seemed to have fallen on deaf ears. But it seemed wrong to stand by and do nothing. GiGi was a good woman, a wonderful woman, who'd raised Antonio after his mother left his dad—left *him*. They had had visits with his mother, but they were few and far between. Because she was an alcoholic, his dad preferred that she come to Italy to spend time with him, but she liked the privacy of her own home. Probably to hide her drinking.

She rarely came to see him, and his grandmother had become a mother to him. Gretta Salvaggio hadn't asked for anything in return. She just wanted her grandson to be happy. Unfortunately, in her way of thinking, happy meant married—with children. She believed children made life worth living.

He thought of his defunct marriage and rolled

his eyes. After the first six months, there had been nothing happy about it.

"Have you ever thought of doing something like that?"

Antonio's blood ran cold. Clearly June hadn't seen the eye roll. "You mean propose?" Dear Lord, he hoped she wasn't hinting. They'd gone out four or five times in the past six months. They weren't really a couple. They were...

They were...

They were...

Friends with benefits?

She also knew he had other "friends." She had to. They didn't keep in touch when he returned to Italy after his appointments with the law firm where she worked. He only called her when he came to the city.

They were casual.

And if this was "the" conversation about where this relationship was going, then he'd have it. "You know I don't believe in marriage."

She sniffed.

He frowned. "Do *you*?"

She shrugged. "Sure. Someday. But I love romantic gestures like that proposal."

So that's what she was hinting at. She wanted a little romance.

He was about to make a mental note to do something romantic, something that didn't spell commitment, when he saw the newly engaged couple leaving the restaurant, stealing kisses as they walked to the door. It struck him that he'd never see them again. He would have no way of knowing if they ever actually got married.

Neither did any of the other people in that restaurant. All they saw was a proposal.

His brain woke up and quickly drew some conclusions. He didn't ever want to remarry, but his grandmother was old-fashioned. She wanted him married. Settled. Preferably with children.

But looking at that couple, he realized he didn't have to get married to make GiGi happy, to give her a burst of energy that would get her moving to schedule her treatments. All he needed was a really romantic proposal that she could see—or watch on YouTube.

YouTube.

He laughed out loud.

"What's funny?"

"My grandmother is sick."

June looked at him as if he were crazy. "What?"

"I'm sorry. I don't mean to sound flip. My grandmother is having some health problems and I just figured out something that will raise her energy enough that she can go through treatment."

June's face scrunched in continued confusion. "Okay."

He knew his explanation had been vague, but that was because he didn't talk about personal things with casual dates. Still, his plan was a good one. He adored his grandmother. She'd been depressed since Antonio's grandfather's death. But the cancer diagnosis seemed to have sucked the very life out of her.

And now he had the plan to revive her.

He rose. "There's something I have to do." He glanced around for the nondescript brunette in the beige skirt. "You can take the limo back to your apartment."

She stood up and leaned against him seductively. "Will you be joining me?"

"Sorry. This thing I'm thinking about might take a while." He kissed her. "By the time I could get to your apartment you'd be asleep. I'll see you next time I'm in town."

She smiled prettily. "Okay. Thanks for dinner."

She headed for the door. Not angry. Not upset.

Their relationship really was the epitome of casual. Still, he decided to send her flowers in the morning. He glanced around looking for the brunette again. He found her in the foyer near the maître d'.

"Good evening."

Gathering her purse and briefcase from the bench by the door, she looked over at him. "Good evening."

"Are you a party planner?"

She studied his face. Maybe gauging his sincerity? But all he saw were her eyes. Green. Not brown-green, but real green. In a face that could only be described as classically beautiful. Pert little nose. High cheekbones. Full lips.

"Yes and no. I plan marriage proposals mostly."

"There's market enough that you can be that specific?"

She sighed. "It's a big city."

"I know." He couldn't believe he was asking stupid questions but just looking at her made him feel funny—like a guy who could trip over his own feet. Which was ridiculous. Italian billionaires raised on vineyard estates were suave. *He* was suave.

"I'm sorry. I just saw that guy ask his girlfriend to marry him and it was pretty clear you'd set it up. I'd like for you to plan a proposal like that for me."

Her face brightened. "Oh! I'm sorry. I thought you were about to ask me to rent a bouncy castle for a bunch of five-year-olds."

He laughed. "No. I have no children." But at thirty-three he could be a father. Which was why his GiGi was always hounding him. She said time was passing him by.

He shook his head to clear it. What the hell was happening with him tonight?

She smiled apologetically. "Don't get me wrong. Kids are great. Kids' parties are fun. But it's been a long day for me."

It gave him a little comfort that they had both gotten off on the wrong foot.

A group of diners arrived, bringing warm June air in with them. Realizing they were standing in everybody's way, Antonio said, "Can I walk you to your car?"

"I've got a ride share coming."

He pointed at the door. "Can I wait with you outside?"

"Why don't you just come to my office first thing tomorrow? I'm in at seven and I don't have anyone scheduled until nine o'clock." She handed him her sedate, classy business card.

Riley Morgan
Making Wishes Come True
Remember your proposal forever

He handed her one of his business cards too, but he winced. "Sorry, that card's got my company information on it, and we're headquartered in Italy. But I'm staying at the Intercontinental. If something comes up tomorrow morning and you can't see me, you can reach me there. I'll want to reschedule. This proposal is very important to me."

She smiled as she tucked his card in her pocket. "Trust me. I can help you figure out the absolute best way to propose to your girlfriend."

"Oh, it's not for my girlfriend. It's for my grandmother."

She frowned. "You're asking your grandmother to marry you?"

"No, my grandmother is ill, and I want the kind of proposal that will make her so happy she'll find the energy to fight."

Her eyes widened, then filled with sincerity. "I'm so sorry."

The softness in her voice warmed his chest. She was pretty, polite, sweet and so sincere it was affecting him in the oddest ways.

He tapped her business card against his hand. It was time to get the hell away from her and gather his wits. The proposal idea was perfect. He wouldn't ruin it because he was acting all wrong, probably because he was tired.

"Since we're meeting so early, maybe we should have breakfast?"

"I'd rather meet in my office. I can show you pictures. We can talk about venues."

"Okay."

She smiled again, so pretty his heart pounded in his chest. The sense that he'd never met anyone like her tried to take over his brain, but he reminded himself he met beautiful women all the time. But this one wasn't as beautiful as she was classic. Like a woodland fairy. Happy and wanting to make others happy.

He shook his head, clearing it of some of the weird thoughts and feelings as he walked out into the warm Manhattan night.

He'd been up for a day and a half. With the time differences he'd gotten to New York almost the same time that he'd left Italy. Technically, he'd gained eight hours in this day. Because of an emergency, he'd worked every one of them even though it was Sunday. He needed sleep. Then he could deal with the pretty green-eyed woman who would help him revive his grandmother.

Riley Morgan left the restaurant glancing at the business card Antonio Salvaggio had given her. She had never met anyone who'd made her feel what he had in a thirty-second conversation. He was gorgeous, dressed like a man accustomed to the finer things and loved his grandmother. That's all she remembered because she kept losing her breath.

She knew why she'd been off balance. When he looked at her, something inside her woke up and demanded attention. That sounded dreamy and romantic and more than a little bit tempting. But when a woman had employees to pay and marriage proposals to plan, she couldn't afford to trip over her own tongue.

She went to bed still chastising herself for losing her cool just because a guy had the accent of a god and the most beautiful dark eyes she'd ever seen—mostly because he'd been with a woman. She'd assumed that was why he wanted a proposal planned.

Actually, she wasn't a hundred percent sure what he wanted.

She finally fell asleep around midnight and woke super early Monday morning with ideas floating around in her head. She dressed in slim pants and a lightweight summer sweater and by the time she arrived at her office, she was absolutely ready to get out the photos and videos of her best events. She made both tea and coffee in the breakroom and had the local bakery deliver a dozen Gourmand pastries.

Her assistant arrived ten minutes later, and she poked her head into Riley's office. "Good morning."

With her flowing red hair and long limbs, Marietta Fontain looked more like a dancer than an office assistant, but Marietta was one of the best.

"Good morning. I have someone coming in in a few minutes. I gave him my card at last night's proposal and told him to stop by at seven."

Marietta smiled. "Okay, boss. I'll be ready."

"You always are. I'll probably be busy with him for an hour. Is there anything I need to know before he gets here?"

"No. I'm putting Vince and Montgomery on the Islee proposal this morning. I haven't yet done the workup of what this proposal entails, but maybe I could do that with them?"

"Good idea. I actually want them to oversee the event itself."

Marietta gasped. "You're taking a day off?"

"No. I'm going to watch from the back of the

venue to make sure they can manage the whole thing on their own."

"Ooh. Clever."

"Don't get your hopes up that training more people means I'll take a day off. I like being at events to make sure everything goes as planned. But you never know what life's going to throw at you. Just in case I ever get sick or need a day off, I want to know all employees can handle an event on their own."

"I love that you think ahead."

"I'm successful because I think ahead."

"Well, thinking ahead is one thing. Doing everything yourself is another. Once those two get up to speed, we'll all be trained. You could trust us for two weeks while you go to the Bahamas or something."

The main door opened. Marietta pivoted to race back to the reception area. "That's my cue."

Riley took a breath. She might have been overwhelmed by Antonio Salvaggio's presence the night before, but this morning she would be all business.

CHAPTER TWO

WAITING FOR MARIETTA to bring Antonio Salvaggio back to her office, Riley took a seat at her desk and pulled up the spreadsheet of that week's schedule. Her company had six proposals. All preplanning had been done. Flowers were ordered. Music had been scheduled. Two violinists. One mariachi band. One string quartet. And two without music.

"Riley?"

She glanced up to see Marietta in her doorway. "Mr. Salvaggio is here to see you."

Antonio Salvaggio stood behind Marietta, smiling. Her stomach fell to the floor.

He was even better looking than she remembered. Today he wore another expensive suit and a smart tie. He was the epitome of a successful businessman, but he somehow made being a businessman look yummy.

"Good morning."

Oh, God, that voice.

She resurrected her smile and rose from her desk. "Good morning."

Marietta scampered away, but turned halfway down the hall and mouthed, *Oh, my God!*

Riley had to swallow a chuckle. "Have a seat."

"Thank you."

As they both sat, she said, "Can I get you some coffee? Tea? A pastry?"

"No. Thank you. I had breakfast at the hotel."

"Then let's get right to your proposal."

"I want something memorable."

"Everybody does." She thought about the woman he'd been with the night before and tried to figure out a way to ask for specifics without reminding him of their clumsy conversation at the restaurant door. "You said the proposal was for your grandmother?"

He shook his head but before he could say anything, Marietta walked in with two cups of coffee. Obviously, her assistant wanted another look at their new client.

"Just in case you change your mind about something to drink."

"Thank you," Riley said as Marietta set the two china cups and saucers on her desk before walking to the door, where she turned and mouthed *Oh, my God!* again.

He took a breath. "Yesterday was a marathon day for me. I'd flown to Manhattan from Italy and spent the whole day with lawyers going over bullet points for a business deal that was falling apart. Which is why I babbled when I tried to explain my idea."

Liking that reasoning, she said, "I had a long day too. I babbled a little myself."

He laughed, his rich voice making the sound deliciously sexy. "My grandmother is depressed. My grandfather died six months ago and she's still grieving. I understand that. But she was diagnosed with breast cancer a few weeks ago and she seems to be ignoring it. When my dad stepped in and instructed her personal assistant to work with the doctor to schedule her chemotherapy, she exploded and refused to go to the appointments. I know this all goes back to her grief, so last night when I saw that proposal you had arranged, I thought of how her fondest wish is to see me married. I don't want to get married, but it hit me that if I did a fake proposal and put it on YouTube, it could excite her enough that she'd come back to life again."

"I see."

His enthusiasm died. "You don't do fake proposals?"

"We haven't to this point, but I don't see why we couldn't do one."

He picked up one of the cups of coffee. "Believe me. I know this probably sounds idiotic, but my grandmother raised me after my parents divorced and my mother returned to Norway. I would do anything to bring GiGi back to her old self at least long enough to get the care she needs."

Her eyes softened along with her voice. "I think that's extremely kind. But how are you going to explain things when you don't actually get married? Won't your grandmother be upset?"

"She's never to find out the engagement was fake. Once she's on the road to recovery, I will simply tell her that things didn't work out with my fiancée. As long as I get engaged in the States to an American girl—someone she doesn't know and won't run into—I don't see how she will discover otherwise."

She sat back. "The idea does make me feel like I'd be doing a good deed."

He nodded and her chest tightened. Good grief. She'd seriously give up her company to see what it would be like to kiss him.

"Don't worry. It might be a good deed, but I'm happy to pay you."

She pulled herself together. "That's not what I meant. You're a good grandson. I totally understand what you're doing and why. I just feel that I need to point out that this might backfire."

"I won't let it. If it does, I'll be the one to deal with it."

The sincerity in his serious dark eyes told her he was as good as his word.

"Okay, then."

"Okay." He shifted on his chair. His smile

warmed again. "Do you have any idea of what we'll do?"

"We can do anything you want. I think if you keep it simple like last night's proposal in the restaurant, your grandmother's more apt to believe it."

"Simple is good. But I was thinking maybe something in Central Park. It's green and lush in June. It would be a pretty space. Also maybe have mandolins playing in the background before I get down on one knee."

"I can do that." She sat forward. "I can also have potted flowers brought in for added color." She thought for a second. "Do you have a budget?"

He laughed. "Spare no expense."

She remembered his suit from the night before, the pretty blonde in the exclusive restaurant, and smiled. "Okay. Let's look at some pictures."

She hit a few buttons on her laptop and pulled up folders of other proposals she had done. She rose and sat on the seat beside him, setting the laptop on her desk between them so he could see what she had.

Opening one of her Central Park proposals, she said, "I like the idea of doing it in a pavilion." She glanced at him to see his reaction and when their gazes met something like lightning shot through her. They were close enough that she could touch him, and she swore she could feel the heat of his body—

She looked away and clicked on a picture of a proposal in Dene Summerhouse, reminding herself that he might be planning a fake proposal, but he had been having a cozy little dinner with a pretty blonde the night before. This attraction was totally one-sided or wishful thinking.

"As you can see, the gazebo itself is a little stark. So, I'd bring in pots of flowers for color." She pointed at the second picture. "We can have the mandolin players over here. And depending on whether or not you have a long speech planned—"

"I don't. As you said, the simpler the more believable."

"Then the whole thing can take two minutes. Unless you'd like to add a dance at the end."

"At the end?"

"After you propose, it would be romantic to share a slow dance. Particularly since you're already bringing in musicians."

"I like it. My grandmother would definitely think that was romantic and we'd still keep the whole thing under five minutes."

He smiled at her, and her nerve endings crackled. She could smell his cologne. If she moved her arm just a fraction their elbows would brush—

She cleared her throat and looked away to break the connection. "Okay. So, all we need is the when."

"I'm leaving town Wednesday morning. If we

do it tomorrow night, could we have it up on the internet by the time I get home?"

She carried her computer back to the correct side of her desk and glanced at her calendar. "I don't see why not. Our proposal tomorrow is in the afternoon. The evening is open." She smiled her professional smile. "Once it's recorded it's only a few clicks on a keyboard to get it up on-line. I can probably text you the link right then and there. Unless you want the video edited. Then you won't have it until morning."

"No editing. I think the more honest the video, the more my GiGi will believe it. She'd love it if there was some kind of blunder. It would tickle her and probably make it even more believable. In fact, maybe we could slide one in."

She shook her head. "We'll keep it simple, but no deliberate blunders. Even if it is a fake proposal, I have a reputation to maintain." But the reminder that he really wasn't getting engaged rippled through her—

She squelched it. The man lived in Italy. She lived in Manhattan. Plus, he was one of those strong, decisive types. She liked sensitive lovers.

She almost slapped herself upside her head.

Why the hell was she thinking these things?

He rose. "Okay. We'll see you tomorrow night then."

"Yes." She hesitated but only for a second. All this had gone too easily. She ran down a mental list of what she needed and basically their short conversation had covered all the bases. Still, given that he really wasn't getting engaged, she couldn't assume he was a lovesick puppy who would do the normal prospective groom things.

"Don't forget to bring a ring."

He laughed.

"I'm serious. It's the most important part of the proposal. Putting the ring on your fake fiancée's finger will be ninety percent of the believability. I also want you to remember that there needs to be some longing glances and a good kiss right after you put the ring on her finger."

He snorted and raised his eyes to the heavens. "Got it."

She didn't want to insult him by telling him to practice the longing glances or the good kiss. She'd seen him kiss the woman at the restaurant. Even if she would only be his fake fiancée, Riley knew Antonio Salvaggio knew how to kiss.

She felt a few seconds of honest-to-God jealousy for the pretty blonde who would be standing in as his fiancée, if only because of that kiss, but stomped it out. She handled her love life the same way she handled her business. Carefully. Intelligently. A fling with a hot Italian guy might get her motor running but without the proper preplanning or thought, it could really blow up in her face. The same way this proposal could blow up for Antonio if they didn't do everything correctly.

She would get her head in the game and make this proposal beautiful and romantic...

And believable.

After Antonio left, her mom stepped into her office. Short and sweet but with a bit of a bossy side, Juliette Morgan sat on the chair Antonio had just vacated. "And who was that?"

This is what happened when you shared workspace with your mom's home nursing agency because rent in Manhattan was so high.

"A customer."

Her mom groaned. "Too bad. That guy is gorgeous."

"And he's from Italy. Too far away to date."

"So, you thought about it?"

She laughed. "Mom, I'm planning the man's proposal."

"Fake proposal," Marietta said as she entered Riley's office.

Riley gasped. "Marietta! That's not supposed to get around."

"Your mother's a nurse. She knows all about confidentiality."

Her mom studied her before she said, "I do know all about confidentiality, but I've also never seen that look on your face before."

"And I told you. He's from Italy. Here on business. I am never going to see him again."

"Except on Tuesday night for the proposal," Marietta interjected.

Her mom examined her for a few more seconds. "I came in here to ask you to have dinner with me on Tuesday night. I guess that's out of the question now."

Riley glanced at her calendar. "Not if we make it a late dinner. What's up?"

"Just some doctors I'm wining and dining for referrals."

She groaned. "They're not single are they, Mom?"

"No. Old and settled. But it's simply better to have you at dinner to keep the conversation from getting too boring." She sighed. "I hate to sound like I'm old and cantankerous, because I'm only fifty, but sometimes these dinners are so dull I could weep."

Riley laughed. "Got it." She pointed at her mom but spoke to Marietta. "If you want to bug someone about taking a vacation. She's the one you should be bugging."

Juliette sighed. "I do not need a vacation. I just need someone to help me keep dinner light and amusing on Tuesday. Can you come?"

"Proposal is at seven, while it's still light out. It's going to be simple, and the client wants one take. He thinks bloopers will make it more believable." She shrugged. "I can be at the restaurant at eight. Eight-thirty at the latest."

Her mom rose. "Good." She walked toward the door but stopped and faced Riley again. "Wear something pretty. Not those beige pants and sweaters you always wear. We're going to The Milling Room. You'll need to fit in not blend into the woodwork."

Riley laughed even though it meant she'd have to bring something fancy to work and change before the Salvaggio proposal, so she wouldn't waste time going home after it. But that was fine. She and her mom had struggled after her dad died. His parents evicted them from his condo, and they were always two steps away from being homeless. All that time, her mom had gone without so Riley could have things. Then she'd started her home nursing agency and taught Riley that having control of your destiny was the only way to go. Now, Riley was a business owner too.

She owed everything to her mom. If Juliette wanted Riley to wear a pretty dress, then she would wear a pretty dress.

Because of the tight deadline, Riley had taken charge of the entire Salvaggio proposal herself. Twenty minutes before she had to leave, she slipped into a pink lace dress for her mom's dinner. She pulled her hair out of the bun and styled it around her shoulders before applying extra makeup and sliding into white sandals.

Clipboard in her big purse, she raced to the lobby to catch the cab that would take her to Central Park. Just off Fifth Avenue, Dene Summerhouse was easy to enter and just as easy to leave, so Riley wouldn't have any trouble getting to the dinner with her mother.

As she was overseeing both the flower arrangements and the mandolin players, Antonio Salvaggio walked up the path to the gazebo. He looked mouth-wateringly handsome in a light-colored suit with a pale blue tie. Both of which accented his dark good looks.

She greeted him warmly. "The blue tie is perfect. It works with your coloring and will show up on the video."

He glanced around the big gazebo. "For as quickly as we planned this, everything looks great."

"As we discussed, this is a simple proposal. You could have gone crazy with music and singing judge choirs or had the cast of a Broadway play sing a love song."

He laughed.

"But we decided on simple."

"Yes." He caught her hand and held her gaze. "Thank you."

Electricity skittered up her arm. With all that sincerity focused on her, his touch could have made her stutter. She forced herself to pull herself together and be professional. "My bill's already in your e-mail inbox."

He snickered and let go of her hand. "I still appreciate it."

She surveyed her crew and the pavilion. "Everything's ready. Do you have the ring?"

He patted his jacket pocket. "Right here."

She didn't need to see it to check off that item on her list. He was clearly organized and thorough, going at this like a businessman. "Do you know what you're going to say?"

"Just 'I love you. Will you marry me?'"

She nodded. "Short and sweet. Exactly what we want. So, where's the bride?"

He frowned. "Bride?"

"Sorry. Where's your fiancée?"

He continued to look at her as if he didn't understand.

"The woman you're going to ask to marry you."

His mouth fell open a little bit. "I thought you were bringing her."

"I don't even know who she is."

"That's the point. There is no one. So just like the flowers and the mandolin players I thought you'd provide someone to fake propose to."

This time her mouth fell open. "I assumed you'd bring the woman from the restaurant."

He squeezed his eyes shut. "No."

"Okay," she said, thinking on her feet. There were three cute young women arranging the flowers, but they were dressed in dark trousers and golf shirts with a florist logo on the breast pocket.

"I…" She looked around.

He tapped her shoulder to bring her attention

back to him. "You're here." He looked down at her dress. "And you're dressed for it."

Damned if she wasn't. She squinted as she thought about her mom telling her to wear a dress—

She couldn't—

She wouldn't—

Could her mom have set up a dinner just to get her to wear a dress to this fake proposal?

She couldn't have. She wouldn't have known Antonio didn't have a fiancée. Still, it wouldn't be the first time Juliette had tried to matchmake.

Antonio's voice brought her back to reality. "Please. We've gone to all this trouble already."

She took a breath. "You're right. It's no big deal and technically I am dressed for it."

"And you look beautiful."

Her heart fluttered before she could remind herself that he'd only told her that because he wanted a favor.

She forced a smile, then turned to Jake, the videographer. "I'm going to be playing the part of the fiancée," she said, holding her smile in place as if it was no big deal that she was standing in for the role. Because it wasn't. This was a job. Period. Nothing more.

"Once I get to the center of the gazebo, you start filming." She faced the mandolin players. "Same instruction to you. Once I get to the center of the gazebo, start playing. I want the video to begin with me standing there, waiting for my Prince Charming with music in the background."

The three guys nodded. Jake scrambled to get into position for the best angle for the simple video.

She handed her big purse and clipboard to one of the flowerpot positioners. The woman looked confused, but she took them.

Riley started up the stairs but stopped suddenly. She faced Antonio. "I'll walk to the center and turn around. Jake will start filming. The guys will start playing. Count to five, then walk up the stairs and meet me in the middle."

He nodded.

She took a long breath and put her forced smile on her face again. She walked to the center and turned.

Jake said, "Action."

The mandolins sent romantic music wafting through the gazebo.

Antonio started up the steps. He walked to her, got down on one knee and took her hand.

When his warm fingers wrapped around hers, she had to work to stop her heart from pounding. The man was simply too darned good looking and sexy.

"I love you, Riley Morgan. Will you marry me?"

The words rippled through her as if they were real. Their gazes held. It was like living a fantasy—

But that's all this was. Fantasy. A fake proposal

to make his grandmother happy. His motives were good. She was getting paid.

Having seen the reactions of hundreds of prospective brides, she smiled broadly and said, "Yes! Yes! I will marry you! I love you too!"

He took the ring from his pocket and slipped it on her finger.

Had she not been fully immersed in the role she was playing she might have taken a second to gape at it. The diamond was huge. The gold band glittered like the sun.

He rose and caught her around the waist and a realization froze her breathing. She'd told him he had to kiss his new fiancée. But that was before *she* was the fiancée.

Their gazes caught. Time went to slow motion as his face got closer and closer. The breath in her lungs shivered. A tremor ran through her. But her stalled brain finally woke up.

Hadn't she thought she'd give up her entire company for one kiss from him? Well, this was her moment.

Her eyes closed. His mouth brushed hers. She swore she heard the choir of judges from Sunday night's proposal singing the alleluia chorus. His lips were surprisingly soft and amazingly experienced. He brought her closer, making her realize she was all but frozen with shock. She slid her hands up to his shoulders, then slipped them around his neck.

As his clever mouth worked its magic, he brought her closer again. Her breasts bumped his chest. All the air disappeared from her lungs.

The mandolin players shifted songs, as they had been instructed, and the music for their slow dance began. He broke the kiss but instead of moving away from her, he stared into her eyes. She saw his confusion and knew it mirrored hers. Every part of her body was warm and tingling. She could have caught his shoulders and brought him back to kiss him again.

But he slid one hand around her waist and took her other hand to lead her in the dance. They drifted together slowly. Even as every cell in her body wanted every second she could get pressed against him, her brain reminded her this wasn't real.

This wasn't real!

Good grief! They were being videotaped for his grandmother. And she was not acting the part of a happy new fiancée. She was shell-shocked.

She stepped closer to him, laid her head on his shoulder familiarly and almost swooned when the feeling of being pressed against him stole her breath again. Temptation skittered through her. For the remaining two minutes, he was hers to cuddle or kiss or—

Stop.

Seriously.

Laying her head on his shoulder was intimate

enough. Especially when his hand drifted from her waist to the middle of her back. The romance of it flitted through her. She told herself one more time that this wasn't real, but the sigh that stuttered out of her was very real.

He was probably the sexiest guy she'd ever met, and they were snuggling. She was allowed to sigh.

It would be good for the video.

CHAPTER THREE

THE MUSIC STOPPED and they broke apart slowly. For the next ten seconds they held each other's gaze. He didn't know what she was thinking but he'd never felt the sensations that had rippled through him when he kissed her. The logical part of him knew his honest reaction would be good for the video, but the male in him was nothing but confused.

He knew all about attraction and seduction. What had happened between them had been... different.

Jake yelled, "Cut!" bringing Antonio's attention to the young man in jeans and a sloppy shirt. He shook his head as he watched the playback on the recorder in his hand. "I think it's perfect."

"I'd like to see it," Riley said, her voice crisp and professional.

Still a bit shell-shocked, Antonio whispered, "I'm pretty sure it's exactly what we want."

His whisper accurately depicted what he felt. A soft, insistent confusion. When he reminded himself this wasn't real, his soul rebelled, confusing him even more. What he'd felt holding her could be as dangerous as it was romantic and wonderful. He'd lost control of that kiss. Following those feelings could mean losing control in bigger, more important ways. Antonio Salvaggio did not lose control. He'd done that in his first marriage, and it nearly destroyed his faith in humanity. Which was what made his reaction so confusing. He knew better.

Jake sauntered over. Addressing Riley, he said, "I texted the video to your phone."

She took her purse from the wide-eyed florist helper who had been holding it and rummaged for her phone. As she pulled it out, it pinged with a text. Two screens later she and Antonio were huddled around it watching the video.

He could see every emotion on her face. Fake surprise when he asked her to marry him became real surprise when he pulled her close to seal the deal with the kiss, which started slowly and built to the unexpected passion that had left him flummoxed. When they'd pulled away, he saw real longing in her eyes. His grandmother would probably see it as romantic. For a second, he did too.

But romance was a mirage. The truth was they'd surprised each other with that kiss. They really were attracted, but they would never see each other again, and these feelings were fleeting. Plus, he couldn't really be upset about never again seeing a woman he only just met. He didn't miss his lovers when they were apart. How could he feel a ping of disappointment over a woman he'd kissed for a video?

When the video ended, he quietly said, "It's perfect."

She smiled at him, back to being totally professional. "It is. I'd say we're done here."

He glanced at Jake. "You'll put it up online?"

"Whatever platform you want."

"Make it private on YouTube—" He didn't want the entire world having access to a fake proposal and he suspected Riley wouldn't either. "I'll send my grandmother the link." Needing to get things back to normal, he shook Riley's hand and smiled at her. "Thank you."

Her face remained professionally pleasant. Though he thought that should jerk him back to reality, it was difficult to pull his gaze away from her.

When he realized he was standing there, holding her hand like a man bewitched, he dropped it. "Good-bye, Riley Morgan."

"Good-bye, Antonio Salvaggio."

He headed out of the park to the limo that awaited him. "Airport, Simon."

His driver said, "Yes, sir. But I thought you weren't going home until morning?"

He laughed. "Have you ever had one of those moments when you knew deep down it was time to go home?"

"Only with a woman I shouldn't have been dating, Mr. Salvaggio."

Antonio laughed. "That pretty much sums it up. Let's get me out of here."

After watching Antonio disappear down a path that would take him away forever, Riley got to work directing the florist's crew to gather the flowers. The musicians packed to leave. Jake headed back to the office to go over the video again to make sure there were no odd things in the background before he put it up on the internet.

The mandolin players left next. Then the florist's helpers carried out the potted flowers and suddenly she was alone.

She glanced around. Technically, she was done and Antonio Salvaggio, good kisser that he was, was out of her life. She blew out a relieved breath and headed out of the park, but the sun caught her left hand and the enormous diamond winked at her.

She froze.

He'd forgotten to take back the ring!

Or she'd forgotten to give back the ring.

Damn it!

She was not walking around Manhattan wearing what she was certain was a million-dollar ring on her finger! She had to return it to him.

She quickly called her mom. The call went to voice mail, which was good. Because when she didn't arrive for dinner, her mom would check her phone and find the voice mail and Riley wouldn't have to make a long explanation.

"Sorry, Mom. I can't make dinner. The proposal took an unexpected turn and I have to fix it."

There. That gave her mom enough information that she wouldn't make her doctors wait for dinner.

She took a cab to her office and pulled up Antonio's file on her laptop. Thank God she had his hotel information as a way to contact him. She quickly called the front desk, and they connected her to his room.

No answer.

She attempted to reach him for an hour and eventually gave up. He could have gone to dinner or a club—or on a date with the blonde.

She winced, telling herself that was none of her business. Getting this ring back to him was.

With the hotel number in her phone, she tried three more times on the cab ride to her apartment. When she used her left hand to open the door, the damned diamond winked at her again. Sighing, she dropped her purse on a living room chair. If nothing else, she could take the darned thing off.

She wrapped her fingers around the slim band to pull off the ring, but it didn't budge.

Groaning, she tried again. Nothing.

She took a seat to give herself better leverage

and pulled one more time. Nope. Not even moving, let alone sliding off.

She tried three times, but it wouldn't come off. It was stuck.

Using an old trick she'd learned from her mom, she put a little cooking oil around it and tried again. It didn't budge.

Tired and more than a little annoyed, she left it on while she showered, put on pajamas and slid into bed. She tried Antonio's hotel room one more time, then remembered she had his business card. Surely, his cell number would be on that.

She whipped it out of her purse only to discover his cell wasn't on it, only the number for his office in Italy. Seeing that, she remembered that was why he'd given her his hotel information. The business card was no help.

She sighed again and eventually fell asleep, though the ring weighed down her finger like a bolder.

Waking early, she dressed quickly and headed to his hotel. At the desk, she said, "I need to see Antonio Salvaggio. Can you call his room for me?"

The clerk hit a few keys on her computer and frowned. "He checked out."

"He checked out? Already? It's not even seven o'clock!"

The clerk looked at her computer screen. "He called last night and said he wouldn't be returning. Housekeeping is packing his things to ship to him."

She stared at the clerk. "He left last night?"

With a sigh of annoyance, the young woman said, "Yes."

"So, if I had something to give him like a signed contract—" She shifted the truth a bit because she couldn't go around with a million-dollar ring on her finger, and she also couldn't drop it in the mail. She knew the hotel had his information. If not his cell number, an e-mail. If he was still in New York, a signed contract could cause the clerk to contact him. "You wouldn't be able to give it to him?"

"Not really. Unless you want me to fly to Italy."

"You don't have a cell phone number?"

"We have his office number…the reservations were made by his company."

Disappointment overrode the clerk's complete lack of concern. "Okay. Thank you." The clerk might not have to fly to Italy, but it looked like she would.

Forty minutes later, her mom sat across from her in her office, sipping coffee in between guffaws of laughter. "I'm sorry, sweetie, but that whole thing about a fake proposal was bizarre."

"It made perfect sense, Mom. His grandmother is still depressed over losing her husband and now she's facing chemo. He knows the video will cheer her up."

"He does realize he's going to have to do a lot of lying over the next few months."

"Not my problem." She waved her hand in dismissal and the ring shimmered in the morning light as if laughing at her. "My problem is getting this stupid ring back to him."

"That's hardly a stupid ring. It's gorgeous. And you're not going to be able to drop it in the mail."

"I know."

"There are services though. You know, delivery companies who handle special packages."

"There are only two problems with that. I can't get it off my finger and I don't want to have it removed by a jeweler for fear we'll damage it. If we have to have a jeweler remove it, I want Antonio with me while they cut the band."

"Looks like you're going to Italy."

She groaned. "I can't! It's a busy time for me."

"I hate to break to you, but the quicker you get to Italy, find the guy and get to a jeweler together, the better."

Riley covered her face with her hands.

"Oh, come on. You're the only person I know who could grouse about going to Italy. Especially when you've been talking about expanding. You say you want to offer proposals in Tuscany, but you don't have any contacts. So go to Italy. Make the contacts with the florists and vineyards and violinists."

She opened her fingers to peek at her mom. "I do want to expand."

Her mom rose from her seat, taking her mug of coffee with her. "Yeah, you do. Why not make your airline ticket open ended? Once you get there you can contact Antonio about the ring, then check out vendors and venues. In between phone calls and meetings, you can take in the sites. Maybe meet a good-looking guy and have some fun."

She snorted. "I might take a few days, but only for work."

"Take some extra time to relax."

"No."

"Why not? You have a very capable staff. Put Marietta in charge. She's been training for this since the day you hired her."

It was true. All the staff had been trained and Marietta could stand in for Riley for a day or two…a week or two really.

Not that Riley intended to take extra days, but this was a really good opportunity to do the legwork she needed to do to expand her business.

She shook her head, then turned to her computer so she could look up Antonio Salvaggio. She had the number for his office in Italy, but what was the point in calling? She had to fly to Italy anyway. It would be much easier to just show him the ring and explain that they needed to go to a jeweler.

Luckily, his family was so rich he wasn't merely listed in the general information websites for his family's companies. He was also in several magazine articles that mentioned he lived in the mansion on the family's enormous vineyard with his father and grandmother.

It finally dawned on her that she couldn't go to his house. *She* was the fake fiancée in the video. If she went to his house, she might run into his grandmother. Oh, boy. That would be peachy.

She would have to go to his office.

She called the airline.

The time difference for Antonio's trip home always screwed up his internal clock. He'd slept on the plane but when he arrived home it was time to have dinner with his father and grandmother, who had a million questions. He'd sent them the link to the video proposal at the airport so he wouldn't have to field their reaction calls while he was in the air. Now, it was time to handle the fallout.

He knew enough about Riley that he could give real answers to GiGi. Except he didn't tell her Riley was a *marriage proposal* planner. He'd told her she was an *event* planner. Which, technically, was the same thing.

His father had given him an exuberant slap on the back and both he and GiGi had asked when they would get to meet this woman who'd finally gotten him to see that love was real.

He'd laughed and told them he wasn't sure when she'd be in Italy, though he threw them a bone by conceding Riley was special. But walking into his office on Thursday morning, he'd frowned, flummoxed again about the sensations and feelings that had raced through him when he'd kissed her. That kiss—one fake kiss—was not an indication that the all-encompassing state called love was real. Love was hormones. Love was the fantasy of men who lost control, lost their footing, and let themselves believe a fairy tale because it felt good. And eventually when the happiness died, and they needed an excuse for making a mistake, love was a much better reason than saying they let their hormones get the better of them.

Which was what had happened in his marriage. Sylvia had been a model so beautiful people stopped on the street to stare at her. She'd been soft and sweet. The paparazzi had loved them as a couple.

Then six months into the marriage, the silent treatment had begun, followed by longer and longer separations for her photo shoots and runway shows.

The sad thing was he'd soon become glad when she left and tired when she returned.

When he'd decided they needed to fix whatever was wrong, he'd surprised her by showing up at her latest gig and found her in bed with her favorite photographer.

He'd had six months of happiness and endured six months of her anger and sarcasm only to discover she'd left the marriage long before he'd even known it was over—

His phone buzzed as he sat on the tall-back chair behind his desk. He answered on speaker.

"There's a Riley Morgan here to see you."

He froze. "Riley Morgan?"

"From New York."

Their kiss popped into his head, along with the sensation of running his hand from her waist up her back and down again. He knew what she tasted like. Knew what she felt like. And wished he'd had the foresight to run his fingers through her hair. He liked it down, not in that bun at her nape. She looked ethereal—

Stop.

He pulled himself together, shoved all that nonsense out of his head. "Please send her in."

Twenty seconds later his door opened and his assistant escorted Riley Morgan into his office. Today she wore jeans and a simple top. She should have looked relaxed and comfortable. Instead, she caught his gaze with wary eyes.

No one ever looked more beautiful.

He thought of his ex. One of the most stunning women in the world. And he reminded himself beauty was only skin deep.

"Thank you, Geoffrey."

His assistant left. He and Riley stared at each other.

Finally, she said, "We have a problem."

This he could handle. "No. We don't. Whatever happened on your end, my grandmother is glowing, and my dad's the happiest I've ever seen him. Fix whatever is wrong because we're good here."

She held up her left hand and the diamond he'd slipped on her finger sparkled at him.

He'd been so confused he'd forgotten the ring.

The oddest rattle of happiness raced through him. She'd brought the ring to him herself? Almost like an excuse to see him.

Try as he might to sound businesslike, his smile ruined it. "You could have found a courier."

"I can't get it off."

His gaze fell to the ring. "Oh!"

"I tried the easy stuff. But I think a jeweler is going to have to cut it off. Since it's clearly expensive I didn't want to go to that extreme without your approval."

Motioning for her to take a seat, he tried to think of something clever to say and couldn't. Too many things buzzed around in his head. Complete lack of concern for the expensive ring. Disappointment that she hadn't been looking for a reason to see him again. And the oddest spike of interest that she'd be in Italy at least for the day.

They could go to a jeweler, get the ring removed, have lunch somewhere romantic—

"Do you have a jeweler?"

He snapped himself back to the present. "Of course. A man doesn't have a grandmother whose birthstone is a diamond without having a jeweler who has a file on everything she already owns."

Riley laughed. "You know there's a part of me that would like to get to know this woman. Not only is she taking charge of her own life, but she got you to fake a proposal and now I find out she gets her own way on jewelry too."

He settled back into his chair. "Yeah, she does."

"Sounds like a firecracker."

He caught the gaze of her stunning green eyes, felt the connection of being in cahoots with each other, as well as having kissed and danced. Complicated, unwanted pleasure filled him again. For as much as he was curious about why he kept experiencing things with her that he never had before with another person, he also did not like things he couldn't explain.

So, no romantic lunch.

Trip to the jewelers, yes.

Lunch? No.

If he was smart, he'd drive her to the airport immediately after they got the ring off and send her home.

"She is definitely a firecracker." He reached for his phone. "Let me call Rafe," he said referring to his jeweler. Before he had a chance to hit the contact number, his office door burst open and his short, wiry GiGi burst in. Dark hair peppered with gray, and a bright red pantsuit made her look like the firecracker Riley guessed she was.

She gaped at Riley. "It's true! You *are* here!"

Riley's gaze jumped to his. He jumped out of his chair. "GiGi! What a nice surprise!"

"I was early for my hair appointment," GiGi said, examining Riley as she walked over to her. "And I thought I'd stop in to kill some time. When I got here, Geoffrey told me you had someone in your office. After I prodded, he admitted it was Riley. So lovely to meet you, dear."

Riley cautiously rose from her seat. "If I'd known I was going to meet you, I'd have worn better clothes."

GiGi's head tilted. "You look comfortable."

"Well, the flight from New York is long. I wasn't about to wear heels."

GiGi laughed. "You missed my Antonio." She patted Riley's cheek. "How sweet…and roman-tic."

Grateful, Riley had kept up the ruse, Antonio said, "And I missed her." He walked over to Riley to slide his arm around her waist. She automatically stiffened, but quickly relaxed.

He frowned. While his entire body filled with happiness at touching her, she'd stiffened?

Not that he cared. He *didn't* care. They were

strangers who'd faked a proposal for his grandmother. Right now, this was all about his grandmother.

Excitement brightened GiGi's pretty face as she said, "Can I see the ring?"

"Of course!" Riley held out her hand. "It's beautiful, isn't it?"

GiGi's eyes filled with tears and every moment of discomfort and confusion he'd experienced because of this ruse became worth it.

"It's beautiful." She caught Riley's hand. "And you are beautiful. I feel like I'm looking at a mirage."

"No mirage, GiGi," Antonio said, though he had to fight back a wince at the lie.

She unexpectedly hugged Riley before patting Antonio's cheek twice. "You surprise me," she told him. "But it's the happiest surprise of my life."

She stood on tiptoe and kissed the cheek she'd just patted. "You two can tell me all about it at dinner tonight. I want to hear everything. How you met. When you kept company. How you kept all this a secret."

Once again, Riley picked up the ball. "Well, we haven't actually known each other long. But when something works, you know it."

His grandmother beamed. *"Si!"* She glanced at her watch and headed for the door. "I need to go, or I'll miss my appointment. But I have to say your engagement filled me with joy…and now I've gotten to meet the woman responsible. This is my lucky day!"

She left Antonio's office and silence reigned for a solid minute.

"Actually, what was *lucky* was that you couldn't get the ring off."

Riley snorted. "If the ring had been off, we could have said that I'd come to Italy because I'd had a change of heart and wanted to break the engagement. And the ruse would be over."

"I don't want it to be over, remember? Not until she starts her treatments. Besides, it's perfect. You live in the US so we can go about our lives normally until Gigi is done with her chemo. She hasn't made arrangements for the treatments yet, but from the joyful look on her face when she met you, I saw shades of happy GiGi coming back. She'll make them soon, then I can keep up the ruse here in Italy until she's well again. When I make trips to the US, I'll say the trips are to see you, not merely for business. All you have to do is come to dinner at the vineyard tonight to make the story look legit."

She frowned. "I don't know… It's getting complicated now."

He caught her hands. Electricity shot through him. He worked to ignore it by remembering the important reason he'd planned all this. "Please?"

She took a breath and expelled it quickly. "Since

we're going beyond our original arrangement, how about a new deal?"

Not wanting to be indebted to anyone, he liked that there was something she needed from him. "Anything."

"I didn't just come to Italy to return the ring. I'm planning to expand my business by offering proposals here in Tuscany. Since I'm here anyway, I was going to scout locations, look for vendors, that kind of thing. Can you get me an in with some of the vendors? You know, put in a good word for me so prices don't go through the roof because I'm from the US. Even if you can't do flowers and musicians…what I really need is a beautiful vineyard to host the proposals."

"I could fix it so that you could use *our* vineyard for proposals if you do this favor for me." He smiled again. "At dinner tonight, you could actually see the place. I'll even give you a tour."

Approval lit her pretty green eyes. "All right."

His chest blossomed with happiness that tried to steal his breath. He warned himself that getting too close to her was playing with fire, but he couldn't shake the sense that having real feelings for each other would help them that night.

"You'll pick me up for dinner?"

"Yes."

The warmth that filled him at the idea of spending more time with her should have been a warning to tread lightly. But he was a grown man, not interested in the relationship they were pretending to have. She would be wonderful with his family at dinner. He had no reason to believe otherwise since she'd played her part very well—even when his grandmother surprised them. He would keep his deal about the vineyard, and tomorrow he would instruct Geoffrey to help her find florists and musicians suitable for her business. When she was done with her research, he would send his limo to take her to the airport so she could go home.

There was nothing to worry about.

CHAPTER FOUR

As GOOD AS his word, Antonio arrived at her hotel around six to pick her up. He got out of the white limo to allow her entry and smiled when he saw her, sending her heart rate through the roof.

"You look wonderful."

She glanced down at her simple pink sundress. "This was the only thing I brought that I thought would suit. But I can easily explain to your grandmother that I packed light. I didn't have anything fancy to wear."

"Makes sense." He motioned for her to enter the limo and got in behind her. "Thank you again for doing this."

"You're welcome. But it's not purely a favor. Don't forget your offer about your family's vineyard."

"I haven't. Mostly because it will be good PR for us too."

She peeked at him. "Oh, yeah?"

"The more people who come to the vineyard, the more positive word of mouth we get."

"Your word of mouth is always positive?"

"Our vineyard is exceptional. We have a luxury wine tasting room, but we also have a gazebo for those who enjoy being outdoors."

"Both sound perfect for proposals."

"And if neither of those work for you…there's a cobblestone path along the perimeter of the vineyard. It's beautiful through the summer."

It surprised her that he'd thought this through, but having just planned his own "proposal," he probably remembered what she'd told him as they were flipping through the pages of her venue book.

Satisfied with their deal, she took a breath and watched the scenery go by. Rolling hills, lush with green grass and rows of grapevines told her why people loved Italy.

"This is amazing."

"Are you speaking generally or for your business?"

"Both. It's gorgeous! If I lived here, I'd never leave."

"I feel the same way about Manhattan. I was born and raised in what most people consider paradise. But Manhattan is a paradise too. Wonderful restaurants. Broadway. Central Park. If I lived *there*, I would never leave."

She laughed. "You're saying the grass is always greener on the other side?"

He faced her. "Something like that." He smiled. "We always want what we can't have."

Unexpectedly intimate, the smile sent a shiver

through her which she barely suppressed. If she really thought about this, he was forbidden fruit. That was probably why he seemed so interesting. Adding that to the connection they had because they were doing favors for each other, her emotions went haywire.

Of course, doing favors for each other technically made them friends. Which was a much better explanation for why she was so happy around him.

That conclusion stopped the weird sense that something personal could be growing between them. Yes. Their kiss had been amazing and dancing with him had been like a fairy tale, but now they had an arrangement. A deal. Anything "personal" between them was nothing more than the friendship developing as a result of their deal.

When they arrived at the vineyard, she had to stifle a gasp. Not just at the beauty of the grounds, but also the villa. The spectacular two-story yellow stucco mansion rambled as if sections had been added to the main house, giving it depth and interest.

"It's lovely."

"It's a monster," Antonio said, helping her out of the limo. "It's been in my family for hundreds of years. It seemed every generation built an addition as a way to add their stamp to it. I persuaded my grandmother that we had enough space, and rather than add on, she tore out the original pool and created a patio that's perfect for parties."

She laughed. "I hope you realize, she's a gem."

"I do." He closed the limo door. "Dinner won't be for at least an hour. Not until my father gets home. I should have told you to bring a swimsuit."

"It's probably better you didn't." She hooked her hand around his elbow, making them look like the couple they were supposed to be. "You'd have never gotten me out of the water. I don't take vacations. A pool sounds like heaven right now."

He chuckled, but quickly sobered. "Are you ready for this?"

"Absolutely. We can amuse your grandmother until dinner, eat, and then you can give me the tour of the wine tasting room, gazebo and path. I'll take a few pictures on my phone and shoot them to Jake who'll start a book for proposals in Tuscany. And I'll go back to the hotel."

"Sounds like a plan." He took a breath. "And really, I'm glad I could help. You truly are going above and beyond for me."

They entered the front foyer and she sighed with appreciation. A curved mahogany stairway led to the second floor. A crystal chandelier caught the sunlight.

"GiGi! We're here!" Antonio called, disturbing the sedate elegance.

GiGi appeared at the top of the stairs and descended like the mistress of the manor that she was, her sheer maxi dress billowing around her.

When she reached the bottom, she kissed both of their cheeks. "Let's enjoy the patio."

"I was just telling Riley about your remodel."

"Remodel?" She cut Antonio a stony look. "Rebuild is more accurate. At the very least it's a total redesign."

Antonio removed his jacket and a man in a white coat suddenly appeared to take it before scampering away.

GiGi led the way down a corridor that revealed sitting rooms and a huge formal dining room before they reached French doors. She opened them on an infinity pool overlooking the vineyard. Then she sat on a chaise shaded by an umbrella.

Riley stared. She rarely got out of Manhattan, so she'd never been on such a huge patio. A long row of French doors lined the entire back wall of the house, granting entry to the patio from most of the downstairs rooms. Yellow stones that matched the stucco surrounded the pool.

There were enough umbrella tables and seating areas for a hundred people beside a huge, covered bar. Beyond that was the vineyard. Lush and green. She had no idea where the winemaking facilities were, or the gazebo or the path Antonio had spoken of, but they appeared to be far enough away that her proposal clients wouldn't disturb the Salvaggio family. They probably wouldn't even know they were there. Which was undoubtedly why Antonio felt comfortable offering those spaces for her use.

Antonio glanced around. "It might be a little warm for me out here in a long sleeve shirt."

GiGi waved him off. "Go. Change out of that suit. Dinner will not be formal. In fact, if you want, we can eat out here."

Riley suddenly felt like a peasant in her simple sundress and sandals and worried GiGi had changed their plans for her.

As Antonio left, Riley glanced down at her clothes, wincing. "I packed light."

GiGi laughed. "You look lovely. And we don't have formal dinners unless we have a guest." She sat up. "*You* are family."

Relief filled her and she sat on the chaise beside GiGi's. "This is a beautiful home."

"It's a monstrosity. But it's our monstrosity. It's been in the Salvaggio family forever." She took a slow breath, suddenly moody. "Even though I came here as a young bride and have been here decades, it still feels wrong to live here without my Carlos."

Riley saw the sorrow and grief etched in GiGi's face and remembered the grief her mother had endured after Riley's dad died. "Carlos was your husband?"

She nodded. "You would have loved him."

The French doors opened.

GiGi said, "That was quick."

When Riley turned, she saw Antonio walking out in shorts and a T-shirt. He looked happy and approachable, but so different that she laughed. "Well, that's a side of you—"

He gave her a warning look.

"That I don't see often enough," she finished, pulling back from saying she'd never seen him dressed casually. No matter how new their engagement, a real fiancée would have seen him in much less than a suit and tie.

He walked over, leaned down and kissed her forehead before lowering himself to the chaise on the other side of GiGi.

She knew he'd kissed her because it was something a fiancé would do and told herself not to swoon over gestures of affection. They had a whole night ahead of them.

Antonio grimaced. "I should have gotten some wine before I sat."

"I would love a glass of white," GiGi said.

Not wanting to be trouble, Riley said, "That's good for me too."

Antonio rose and walked to the covered bar. He stowed a bottle of wine in a bucket of ice and set it on a fancy cart. He added four wine glasses, then wheeled the cart to their seating area.

He filled the first glass and handed it to GiGi, then poured a glass for Riley.

Their gazes caught. "Thank you."

"You're welcome."

An unholy sense of rightness rattled through her, but she reminded herself it was simply the connection of doing favors for each other. Not just the ruse but his offer of helping her. They were friends. Business associates.

She took a sip of her wine, as an older gentleman came out of the French doors. Every bit as tall and handsome as Antonio, he headed toward their grouping of chaise lounges.

"Enzo!" GiGi said. She motioned to Riley. "This is Antonio's fiancée."

Antonio rose from his chaise. "Dad, this is Riley Morgan. She's from Manhattan. Riley, this is my dad, Lorenzo Salvaggio."

She rose as he reached her chair, extending her hand to shake his. But the dark-haired gentleman caught her in a bear hug, almost causing her to spill her wine.

"What a pleasure!" he said excitedly, as he released her far enough that he could hold her at arm's distance and study her. He turned to Antonio. "You do the family proud. She is lovely." He faced Riley again. "This also explains how he could keep your relationship a secret! You live across an ocean."

Antonio chuckled. "Surely, you didn't think I flew to Manhattan twice a month just to see lawyers."

His father laughed. Antonio poured him a glass of wine.

"So, you are from Manhattan?"

"Yes. I run an event planning business."

"That's interesting."

Realizing Antonio's father was smart enough to put two and two together if they didn't handle this right, she smiled. "It's a fun challenge. Every event is different. I also have five employees. But if the business keeps growing the way I mapped out in my five-year plan, I'll be adding two more every year."

Enzo beamed at her. "Impressive."

"Thank you."

As if Enzo's arrival was a signal, the kitchen staff quietly began preparing one of the umbrella tables for dinner.

When they were done, Enzo rose from his seat. "It looks like they are ready for us, and I am starving."

"Me too," Riley said, so comfortable with Antonio's family that she should have at least wondered about it, but she didn't. She got along with Antonio, who was basically a stranger. Why wouldn't she get along with his father and grandmother?

They took their wine glasses to the table. As they sat, Antonio went behind the bar for another bottle. A young woman served antipasto.

When everyone was settled, Riley tasted her first bite and groaned. "This is fabulous."

GiGi pointed at her. "I'm thinking you don't eat enough."

She shook her head. "Trust me. I do. I have one

of those metabolisms that runs like a race car. I can and do eat a lot."

"Or maybe it's that you work too much," Antonio suggested.

"I don't think I do," Riley disagreed but it was a great way to continue their conversation about her business, including the fact that she shared office space with her mom, so they didn't touch on anything too personal that might trip them up. She didn't want to make a mistake or lie to his grandmother any more than they already were.

Dinner, Florentina steak and pasta, was served and the conversation about her business continued through the meal. Riley noticed GiGi losing her energy, winding down from the day, and wasn't surprised when she refused dessert.

"I'm just feeling tired." She smiled at Riley. "We talked so much about your company, we haven't heard about anyone in your family except your mom."

"That's because it's just my mom and me," Riley said, setting down her gelato spoon.

GiGi's eyes softened. "I'm so sorry. Your father...?"

"Unfortunately, my father passed when I was seven." Empathizing with GiGi and realizing she might need to know she wasn't alone in her grief, Riley added, "I was a kid, but I still remember the loss like it was yesterday. My mother seemed to grieve forever."

"Si." GiGi nodded. "I understand."

"But she's good now. Her business made her wealthy. She's busy and happy. She flits all over Manhattan like she owns the place."

Everyone laughed.

GiGi said, "What does her husband think about that?"

Confused, she tilted her head. "Her husband? You mean my dad?"

"No, her new husband. She was young when your father died. Did she not remarry?"

"She never married at all." Riley shook her head. "She and my dad lived together after she got pregnant. They believed they had all the time in the world to get married. Turns out they had only eight years together before he died."

GiGi clutched her chest. "That is sad."

"It was, but it was long ago."

"So long that she could have found someone." Serious and solemn, GiGi held her gaze. "Did she never want anyone but your dad?"

Riley had indulged this conversation hoping to help GiGi see that her future wouldn't always be filled with grief. Instead, it seemed she was making GiGi sadder. "What she went through after my dad was rough. She sort of lost her faith in people."

And that was worse.

Now she was going to have to explain why her mother had lost her faith in people. There was no way Antonio's grandmother would relate to the rest of her story.

"Because my parents never married, my father's family refused to acknowledge us. After I was born, my mom went to nursing school. My father paid all household expenses. When my mom got out of nursing school, they kept that up…with my mom using her paychecks to buy things I needed. Meaning, my dad's family believed my mom had no stake or share in the condo he'd bought before they met. Lawyers served us eviction papers two days after he died, and my mom packed and left. She probably could have hired a lawyer to get a piece of his estate. But she didn't want it. She wanted nothing from his family. She had loved him. Not his money. And she saw walking away as proof of that."

GiGi took a breath. "That is romantic and strong."

"Yes, to both."

GiGi rose to leave. "And I understand perfectly."

She did. Riley knew GiGi was a lot stronger than she let on. Though she grieved, there was a strength beneath the sadness. Riley longed to let GiGi pour her heart out about her late husband, but she wasn't really part of this family.

For the first time, the ruse seemed wrong. But she wouldn't let that thought stick. Antonio's fake proposal would ultimately help GiGi.

GiGi studied her for a second before she said, "I'm glad your mamma is happy."

"Yes." The sincerity in GiGi's eyes made her realize again why Antonio didn't want to lose her. She was a wonderful, empathetic person. "Thank you."

Antonio rose from his chair. "I promised Riley a tour of the wine tasting room, gazebo and vineyards." He held out his hand to her. She rose and took it. "We'll be back to say good night."

Enzo rose. GiGi smiled. "I will see you then."

Antonio kept her hand as they walked around a hedge to a hidden cobblestone walkway. The lights for the path shifted from the patio lights to quaint streetlamps.

The "other" side of the vineyard came into view. A huge building with the same yellow stucco as the house sat in front of even more fields of grapevines. A big tree shaded the gazebo. Lit by streetlights, a path wound from the wine tasting room to the gazebo and along the vineyard.

Just as Antonio had told her.

As they grew closer, she could hear the music that billowed out of the building. A parking lot filled with cars and buses didn't exactly ruin the ambience of the beautiful place, but it did show her she'd probably want to use the gazebo or path for proposals.

"I'm sorry that it's noisy, but this is a typical Thursday."

"Oh, don't be sorry," she said, enjoying the moonlight and the fresh air of the vineyard. Realizing they were far enough away that they didn't need to be holding hands, she pulled her hand out of his but wished she hadn't. She'd probably be in Italy another day or two. Was it so wrong to enjoy him while she had him?

She shook her head to clear that thought. She was not really engaged to Antonio. They weren't even dating. They were now business associates, and she would act accordingly.

Pulling her phone out of her dress pocket, she snapped a few pictures that she sent to Jake. "I need to get the real idea of what the area looks like so I can decide how to handle things. The inside might be noisy, but the outside is beautiful. Romantic."

He laughed.

As they approached the gazebo, she took more pictures, then twirled in the moonlight. "This is the place for evening proposals…and the path by the grapevines would be my choice for daytime."

They continued along the cobblestone, long enough for Riley to see the area was dreamy in the moonlight and maybe rethink the path for nighttime proposals, then they headed back to the house.

Antonio led her to a family room where GiGi was reading, and Enzo watched a sporting event on a big screen TV.

"I'm going to take Riley back to her hotel."

GiGi balked. "Why is your fiancée staying at a hotel, not the villa?"

Riley almost choked. But Antonio didn't miss a beat. "It's a luxury hotel and I'm not coming back." He wrapped his arms around Riley from behind. "We're still celebrating our engagement."

Clearly pleased, GiGi smiled, but heat went through Riley. She pictured it. She could see them kissing in her room. He would romantically sweep her off her feet and she would melt like butter—

She stopped the vision, but the yearnings remained. The evening had been warm and happy, their walk romantic.

Going back to her room seemed like a logical next step—

No. It did not!

Thoughts like that shouldn't even enter her mind. Antonio was a stranger—

Well, technically, that was no longer true. She now knew his family. She'd seen his office and part of his home. And while she'd talked to his GiGi, he'd sat back and listened to the story of her life.

They weren't strangers anymore. They knew a lot about each other.

The excuse that gave her a good reason to stay an arm's distance away was no longer true.

She was really going to have to keep her guard up now.

CHAPTER FIVE

WHEN THEY ARRIVED at her hotel, Antonio helped Riley out of the limo. Given that he couldn't go home, he would also have to get a room for the night. This hotel was as good of a place as any.

Stepping inside the plush interior of the pale stucco building, he reminded himself that spending the night in one of the exquisite rooms wouldn't be a hardship, though he wished he'd thought ahead to bring clothes for the next day. Luckily, he had an extra suit in his office closet and could change out of his shorts and T-shirt when he got to work.

"Let's make a quick stop at the reservation desk," he said, directing Riley that way. "I'll need to get a room."

Two steps before they would have reached it, the gentleman ahead of them turned. Antonio's chest pinched, then his father's friend Marco said, "Antonio?"

"Si. Buonasera." He shook Marco's hand.

Glancing at Riley, Marco said, *"Buonasera."*

"Marco, this is Riley Morgan. Riley, this is Marco Ricci. He's a good friend of my father's."

"Your father's *best* friend and your godfather," Marco corrected, reverting to English, as Antonio had done, for Riley's benefit.

Riley said, "It's a pleasure to meet you."

Marco grinned as if he'd caught Antonio in the act of escorting a woman to a room for the night. Then he glanced at her hand.

His gaze jumped to Antonio's. "You are engaged?"

Antonio took a quick breath. He had no choice but to keep up the charade. Marco might live in Paris, but he still did business in Italy with Antonio's father. He slid his arm around Riley's lower back. *"Si."*

"*You* are *engaged*?" Marco repeated, his voice dripping with confusion.

Antonio laughed. "Why are you so surprised?"

"Your first marriage was a disaster."

And the whole world seemed to know.

It was the embarrassment of a mistake that would follow him forever. "Yes. I was there, remember?"

Marco unexpectedly grinned. "I want to tease you mercilessly about breaking your vow to remain single forever, but your Riley, she is beautiful. And, honestly, I am happily surprised."

"So were we," Antonio said, knowing from the look on Riley's face that she was drawing conclusions about him and his life. The way he'd realized things about her and her life while she'd talked to his grandmother. "But really, we need to be going."

Marco laughed. "Too bad. I'm on my way to the bar." He pointed behind them to the lounge with glass walls providing a view of every inch of the lobby. "I would buy you a drink to celebrate."

"We're tired," Riley put in, obviously realizing they didn't want to prolong their conversation with his father's best friend. "But it was a pleasure to meet you."

"Si," Marco said. "It was my great pleasure to meet you too."

With that, he turned and went into the bar, taking a seat right beside the wall of glass that faced the lobby.

Antonio held back a groan. Now for sure he couldn't leave Riley's room until Marco left the bar. There was no way the old man wouldn't see him sitting right by the window!

He guided Riley into the first elevator. As the door closed behind them, she said, "What are you doing?"

"Coming up to your room with you. I had intended to get a room at the desk, but with Marco watching from the lounge I'll just call from your room."

She gave him a skeptical look.

"You have to know Marco can't see me leave or the ruse is ruined."

"And you have to know that if he sees you at

the desk, he could just think there's something wrong with our accommodations."

Antonio sighed. "It's easier for me to call the desk from your room."

She studied his face for a second. "I suppose."

The elevator stopped on her floor. They walked down the hall. She opened her door with her key card.

As they stepped inside, he understood her apprehension. The tingle of attraction that always seemed to whisper through him when she was around tripled as she closed the door—leaving them alone in a bedroom.

Worse, the room was small, barely big enough for the queen-size bed.

Seeing a house phone on a tiny table between two chairs in a corner, he walked over to it. He picked up the phone's receiver and hit the button for the front desk.

Apprehension filled him again. No matter where he stood, he was by the bed. "You certainly got a small room."

She crossed her arms on her chest. "I'm the only one staying in it. All I need is a bed and a place to shower. I'm going to be working, remember?"

The clerk answered his call with a chipper "Front desk."

He sighed with relief. "Good evening. This is Antonio Salvaggio. I need a room for the night."

Riley put her suitcase on the bed and unzipped it. She pulled out something pink and shear—not quite see-through but filmy. Soft and sexy looking.

Were those her pajamas?

If so…wow.

"I'm sorry, sir. We're all booked."

The clerk's comment brought him back to the present and he frowned. "Really?"

The good-natured clerk laughed. "*Si.* If you'd like a room tomorrow night, I could book that now."

"No. I need a room tonight. Isn't there something you're holding in reserve, something I'd happily pay extra for?"

"I'm sorry. Those rooms are gone too. It was a busy day today."

He wanted to argue, then wondered why. He'd seen the crowded lounge. Besides, there were other hotels in the city.

"Thank you." He disconnected the call.

"They're all booked up, aren't they?"

"We should have guessed that from the crowd of people in the lounge." He took a breath and faced her. "I can't go home."

"I know. Luckily, there are other hotels."

"Yes, but I can't go past the bar until we know Marco's not in there anymore."

"Are you sure he'll see you?"

"He's right by the wall of glass." He sighed. "Besides, Marco sees everything. It's why my father likes doing business with him."

"Okay." She glanced around awkwardly. "I guess you're stuck here for a while." She looked around again. "I was going to shower."

"You still can. You going to another room for a while might make this easier."

"I'll be coming out in pajamas."

Yeah. That little pink filmy thing.

Still, as a gentleman, he said, "I won't look."

Pink pajamas under her arm, she grabbed a couple more things from her suitcase and walked into the bathroom.

He sat on one of the chairs by the tiny table. The sound of the shower leeched into the room. He told himself not to think about the fact that she was naked under a warm spray of water…but the picture formed anyway. He could imagine all her soft skin dampened by the warm water. See himself walk up behind her and kiss her neck—

All right. That was enough of that.

He pulled his phone out of his pocket and began looking for another hotel. He didn't call any of them, only got their phone numbers.

The bathroom door opened. He blinked. Either she was the fastest showerer in recorded history, or he'd been scrolling longer than he'd thought.

"That was quick."

"I don't waste time or water."

He narrowed his eyes, squinting to see her better. "Are those yoga pants?"

"Yes."

"And a bra?"

"Yes."

He gaped at her. "Why? I told you I wouldn't look."

"You just looked, or you wouldn't know I was in yoga pants."

He laughed. "You must be really attracted to me to be afraid to put on your pajamas."

She pulled back the bed's comforter. "Yes and no."

He snorted. That was a sort of honest, sort of confusing answer. "Yes and no? You're either attracted to me or you're not."

"You're a very handsome guy. Of course I'm attracted to you."

"But…"

"But I don't want to be."

He shook his head. "That doesn't count. I don't want to be attracted to you either but I still am."

The room grew silent. She sat on the bed, propping her back up with pillows.

All the feelings he kept having around her intensified. He knew she was attracted to him. The proposal kiss demonstrated that. He'd also seen the way she looked at him sometimes. But hearing her say it made it more real. More earthy—more *possible* that something could happen between them.

"I'm not sure I'm glad we got that out in the open."

E-reader in her hand, she peered over at him. "Out in the open means we're both aware this little thing between us exists so we know to ignore it."

He stretched his legs out in front of him, suddenly confused about why they were fighting this. It wasn't like either one of them was committed to anyone else—and they *were* attracted.

"Why, exactly, do we want to ignore it? Right now, my grandmother is very happy, thinking we're spending the night together. And Marco's probably thinking I'm a lucky guy."

"Oh, you're so funny." She dropped her e-reader and snapped off the lamp. The room became dark as midnight. If that wasn't a sign that she wanted him to go he didn't know what was.

"You do realize that I might have to stay in your room tonight."

"And you realize we already decided that's not a good idea."

He dropped his voice an octave. "You're the one who thinks that. My whole thought process has had a radical transformation. We're adults who are attracted. What's the big deal?"

"The big deal is this relationship is going nowhere."

"Does it have to go somewhere? Isn't a night of blistering passion worth it?"

"Seriously? Are you that vain? It might have been a while since I dated anyone, but I still have a head on my shoulders. I can resist you."

He sunk down in the chair. "Good, then there's no reason I can't stay in your room."

Riley stifled a groan, realizing she had sort of walked into that. She pulled the silky sheet up to her chin and huffed out a sigh. If he wanted to sleep on a chair, he was welcome to it. But she was firmly committed to keeping her guard up around him.

Antonio's voice drifted to her in the darkness. "You are perfectly safe. I don't have to accost women. I have a vibrant social life."

A string of jealousy wound through her. Not just jealousy for the lucky women, but for the fact that he was as busy as she was, yet he still found time—and partners. Of course, he was a rich Italian guy with an accent that probably made women swoon. "I believe that."

"What I'm saying is, if you don't want to explore our attraction, I'm fine with it. You have nothing to worry about from me. As my godfather said, I had an ugly divorce. My wife cheated on me and fought to get more of my family's property than she had a right to. And my parents' divorce was even uglier, mostly because my mom is an alcoholic, and my dad got a court order that her visits with me had to be supervised. I've never seen a divorce that didn't result in fights and hatred. So, I stay away from commitments. Now that I know you're the kind of woman who wants to get married, I'll stay away."

The room remained silent for a few seconds as she settled her head on her pillow, not happy with him. She understood that a bad marriage and divorce could sour someone on commitment, but that didn't make him smart enough to figure her out after a few encounters. She might ultimately want to be in a permanent relationship, but she didn't think she wore that like a sign. It annoyed her that he so quickly pegged her as someone who wanted to get married, when she didn't advertise it.

"How do you know I want to get married?"

"You're nice. You were great with my grandmother. So open and easy. Talking about your mother as if my GiGi already knew her." He shrugged again. "You have 'nice-and-kind-and-likes-being-part-of-a-family' written all over you."

She sat up. "That's funny, since the last three guys I dated didn't see that at all. They thought I'd be happy just dating forever. The one guy still lived with his mother before he moved in with me. I think he liked my apartment more than he liked me."

Laughing over her joke about her last boyfriend, he rose from the chair. "I'm getting the spare blanket. There's usually one in the closet."

She rolled her eyes. "It *was* funny that my boyfriend liked my apartment more than me, but it made me realize I attract all the wrong men."

"You're trying too hard. You're beautiful, smart and kind. One day the right guy will see all that."

She couldn't stop her chest from tightening when he said she was beautiful. It wasn't the first time he'd said it. But that only validated the fact that he *really* thought she was beautiful. It took her breath away and made her question making him sleep on a chair just because she knew nothing would come of them sleeping together—

That was when the truth hit her.

He was just like her exes. Except he was smart enough to see that she wanted more out of a relationship than sleeping together and sharing rent.

And maybe that was the warning she needed to get rid of the romantic feelings she always had around him.

Several minutes went by, but try as she might, she couldn't sleep. She flopped to the right, then back to the left.

Antonio's voice again came from across the small room. "So, tell me about your parents—your father's death. It's interesting that your mother never found anyone else. Were they so happy together that it makes you want to find something permanent?"

"Yes and no."

"You really have a tough time making up your mind about things."

"I forgive myself for riding the fence on this issue. My mother put everything into her relationship with my dad. And while I can look back and envy that they had a once-in-a-lifetime love, I saw what happened when she lost that love. She was shattered. The horrible way his family treated her didn't help."

He whispered, "I'm sorry."

"Don't be. As I said, my mom pulled herself together, started her home nursing agency and she is now rich and successful. Happy as a clam."

"So, your reasons for wanting to marry have nothing to do with things you might have missed out on after your father died?"

She sat up and flicked on the lamp by the bed. "That's the confusing part. Even seeing my mom lose my dad, I still want someone in my life. Someone to share my life. You know. Kids. A minivan. A house in the suburbs. Is that so wrong?"

"It isn't exactly wrong, but it might be wishful thinking. The world's a different place than it was when your parents were a couple. Especially since there are much better ways two extremely attracted people could be spending *this* night. And you're letting a fantasy you have prevent us from indulging in an attraction we both feel."

"It's not a fantasy... Lots of people find real love."

"Name two."

"My mother found it with my dad."

He winced. ".You can't use your parents because their romance was cut short. Fate didn't
give them a chance to go the distance."

"Okay, how about my best friend? She lives in
Scarsdale with a man who dotes on her."

He winced again. "It's my experience that men
who do too much are overcompensating for the
fact that they're having affairs."

She gaped in horror at his train of thought.
"What is wrong with you?"

"Nothing."

"Not everybody's as cynical as you are."

"I'm not cynical. I just don't kid myself into
believing in things that don't exist." He took a
long breath. "Go to sleep."

She might not go to sleep, but she was done
talking to him. She flicked off the light again,
fluffed her pillow and flounced to her side. But
before she drifted off, she thought about the three
serious relationships she'd had in the past six
years. Her college love, the first guy she'd lived
with and the guy who wanted to move out of his
mother's house.

If anybody had a right to believe true love didn't
exist, it was her.

Damn his hide for reminding her.

The next morning, Antonio woke to her shaking him.

He'd given up on sleeping on the chair and had

stretched out on the floor. Their conversation the night before had gotten a little intense. He might have even crossed the line in trying to get her to understand that she might be hoping for a fairy tale that wouldn't ever come to pass.

Actually, that could be what all the shaking was about.

He rolled over. "Enough. I'm awake."

He lifted himself off the floor, remembering something Riley had said about how her other boyfriends hadn't seen that she was looking for real love. He'd heard the disappointment in her voice, and he'd hated recognizing her sadness—which is why he'd wanted her to steer clear of believing in something that would always hurt her. Her desire to find something that didn't exist threw up all kinds of red flags for him. She had a successful business, and she was happy. Her idea that she could find real love could actually ruin a lot of life for her.

That wasn't his business. Was it?

No. They were only pretending to be engaged. If they hadn't been forced together for so long the night before, they never would have had the conversation that made her angry. Because they had, he decided they needed to put some space between them. Meaning, he would let his assistant help her with venues and today they would take care of getting the ring off her finger. That would end their time together.

As she walked into the bathroom, he pulled out his phone and called Rafe.

An employee of the jewelry store answered.

"This is Antonio Salvaggio. I need to speak with Rafe…"

"I'm sorry, Mr. Salvaggio. But Mr. Carabot is on vacation for another week."

He sucked in a breath. Okay so they couldn't take care of the ring today. Having Geoffrey help her with her search for vendors would give them sufficient time apart to forget last night's conversation before they had to see each other to handle the ring.

"Thank you. I will call again when he returns."

He disconnected the call and glanced around, looking for his sandals, intending to head to his office. But the guilt he felt about their conversation the night before filled him again. It truly hadn't been his job to change her mind about love and he knew he'd kept talking when he should have stopped. What she wanted—what she believed—wasn't his concern.

He slipped into his shoes.

Walked to the door.

And stopped.

He couldn't just leave. She was doing him a huge favor. She'd been good to his family. He owed her an apology.

He sat on the edge of the bed, waiting for her to

come out of the bathroom. When the door opened, he bounced up.

"Look, before I go, I just want to say I'm sorry. I pushed you last night, trying to get you to see my side of life and that was wrong."

She shook her head. "I get it. I probably seem like a dreamer to somebody who had such a bad divorce."

"Yes! I did have a bad divorce! I *am* jaded. Sometimes that makes me get on a soapbox. I'm sorry."

She studied his face for a few seconds, then smiled. "I forgive you."

His face scrunched in surprise. He'd expected at least a little scolding. Instead, she said she forgave him. "Just like that?"

She chuckled. "Just like that. It's what people do."

Not the people he knew. His ex could have turned this misunderstanding into a month-long pout.

The funniest sensation skittered along his spine. Relief and confusion spiraled together as she held his gaze with her earnest green eyes.

Something fierce rose in him. He wanted to kiss her so bad, his heart thrummed. But he couldn't. Faking things for his grandmother, he could kiss her all he wanted. Having real feelings, he couldn't.

And maybe that was really why he was off balance, pushing when a smart person would back off. Half the time they were pretending. The other half, they were real with each other. He didn't feel like himself either time, and he wanted to be normal with her. Himself. Not a fake fiancé.

He slid his hands to her shoulders, his eyes on hers, watching for signs of displeasure. But he didn't see any as he pulled her to him for a kiss.

She softened like summer rain. Her arms went around his neck. His arms drifted to her waist, pulling her closer. Relief fluttered through him, along with the notion that this was the smartest thing he'd done all week. He couldn't stand the thought that she had been upset by him—or hurt. It gutted him to think he had hurt her. But she'd forgiven him.

He pulled her closer, luxuriated in the feel of her in his arms, but when happiness began to morph into arousal, he pulled away.

"Thank you for being so good to me. I appreciate you helping me with my grandmother. Today I will tell my assistant to make time to help you with vendors. Come by my office whenever you are ready."

With that, he left her room and walked down the hall, feeling like himself for the first time since he'd met her.

Except he'd kissed her.

He might be happy to be back to behaving like himself, but theoretically kissing wasn't allowed.

Particularly since they now knew they weren't compatible. They wanted two different things out of life and the kind of affair he would want with her could hurt her.

Which was why Geoffrey would be helping her with vendors, not him. No matter how attracted he was to her, she wanted the fairy tale. His first marriage showed him it didn't exist, and he wouldn't pretend it did. Which proved they were not a good match.

Not even for an affair.

CHAPTER SIX

AFTER HE LEFT, Riley stood staring at the door. It hadn't surprised her that he'd apologized. His comments about what she wanted out of life had been a step or two over the line. But he'd recognized that and said so. Which put their relationship back on track. Still, that apology was nothing compared to how he could kiss. That kiss had been sexy and breath-stealing—

No. That wasn't what had stolen her breath.

He'd kissed her for real.

His grandmother wasn't around. That kiss hadn't been for the charade. He'd kissed her because he wanted to.

Tingles of possibility tightened her chest. She and Antonio had shared a kiss filled with emotion. A real kiss had sealed his apology and her forgiveness.

She had been correct the night before. They were no longer strangers. Or even friends who'd made a deal to help each other. There was something happening between them.

But he didn't believe in love, and she did.

If she didn't keep her wits about her, they could make a major mistake. One of them or both of them could end up hurt.

She turned away from the door, disappointed that they couldn't explore this. But they couldn't. She wanted real love. Kids. That house in Scarsdale—

Besides, it was best not to screw things up again. After his apology, their friendship was back on track, his assistant would help her find florists, musicians and singers and she would stay away from him before one of them said something else that put his ruse in jeopardy.

She showered, dressed for the day and left the hotel. She'd intended to have breakfast in the restaurant/lounge with the glass wall but at the last minute she remembered Antonio's god-father. She didn't want him to see her eating breakfast alone and she wanted even less for him to join her. Then she'd have to keep up the charade with him. Frankly, she was a little tired of her life being confusing. Now that things had been straightened out, she would avoid walking into trouble.

Except he'd kissed her. For real.

Yeah, but it had been a kiss to seal his apology. Not an attraction kiss.

She ate at a sidewalk café, then made her way to Antonio's office, fortifying herself to see him. For a kiss between friends, it had been awfully sweet and sexy and *emotional*. The sense that there was something brewing between them hummed through her like the music of a favorite song, but she stopped her thoughts, reminding herself that they were in a good place. She would act like a businesswoman when she saw him.

At least she hoped. Her emotions around him were so powerful that it was difficult to control them or even think rationally sometimes. That's why being with him was so confusing. She was an intelligent, logical person yet she still had to fight an attraction that was all wrong.

In the building housing Antonio's office, she took the elevator to the third floor. Antonio's assistant, Geoffrey, jumped out of his seat when she entered. Tall, with dark hair and dark eyes, he didn't look much older than twenty-two.

"Mr. Salvaggio instructed me to find some vendors for you. I took the liberty of letting them know you'd be stopping by and telling them what you were looking for."

He handed her a neatly printed list and she smiled at him. She'd worried for nothing about how she would react to Antonio. He didn't even come out of his office to say hello.

"Thank you. I'm impressed."

"I can come with you to scope out the vendors if you want."

"No. Thank you." She took a breath, telling herself she wasn't disappointed, but she was.

Which was probably why it was better she didn't see him. All the emotion that kiss dredged up would only get them into trouble. Especially since he didn't believe in love.

Yeah. It was better not to see him.

She forced a smile for Antonio's assistant. "I'll call you if I have questions."

"Come back and let me know how everything went. If there are problems or other vendors you'd like to talk to, I can arrange that."

She would not be coming back. "I'm good for now."

She put the list in her purse and headed out the door, telling herself Antonio's apology and her forgiveness were a good way to end their dealings. It was a clean, effective, happy break. He didn't need her to continue the ruse for his grandmother. He could handle that on his own. His assistant had given her the help she needed with vendors. Technically, their business was done. They could both get on with the rest of their lives.

She barely got to the sidewalk before Antonio came running out of the building. "Riley!"

She stopped. He'd changed out of the shorts and T-shirt he'd worn to dinner—and slept in—the night before. He probably had spare clothes in his office—and was back to looking deliciously handsome.

"Antonio?"

"I didn't want Geoffrey to let you go alone."

"He asked if he could accompany me, but I told him I was good on my own."

He shook his head. "No. You are doing me an enormous favor with my grandmother, and you don't know your way around the city. I promised to give you help with vendors." He glanced around, as if thinking through the situation. "It's so beautiful out, I could take the rest of the day off." He peered over at her. "We could have lunch, then look at Geoffrey's list together."

Her heart stuttered. Had he just asked her out? After kissing her for real?

She groaned internally at the juvenile reaction and forced her common sense to the front of her brain. He owed her for playing the role of his fiancée. He was not asking her out. He was paying her back.

After that kiss?

"You don't want me to go with you?"

"I do! Really! I just—"

Just what?

Wanted him to define what they were doing? Wanted him to explain why they were going to lunch together when they didn't have to? They had opposite beliefs. She knew they wanted different things. She shouldn't even be considering what his offer meant. She should take it at face value.

Except she liked him. *That* was the problem. She liked him enough to wish that even one little piece of what was happening between them was real.

That was really why she'd gotten so upset with him the night before. She was looking for something real, and he wanted something insubstantial. He'd offered a night of blistering passion. Which, if she thought about it, was all two people could share when they were only getting to know each other.

But she wasn't a night-of-blistering-passion girl.

And that had been the end of that.

Still, he did owe her the help with vendors, and it probably was a good idea to have him come along so she could find her way without constantly consulting GPS. She'd take his offer for what it was. Payback.

"I'd love lunch."

"Great!" He stuffed his hands in his pockets, and they started up the sidewalk. "If I know Geoffrey, he's got Spinelli's Flowers on that list. They're actually just up the street. Maybe we'll pop in there before we eat."

"Okay."

She said it happily, like someone grateful for his assistance, but walking together like business friends felt odd. Awkward. Not normal.

Actually, *this* was their real normal. Everything else that had happened between them was either for the fake engagement or in a bedroom where they were feeling two different things. Right now, he was thanking her for helping him and she would appreciate it.

The muffled sound of a phone ringing floated to her from her purse, interrupting her thoughts.

"That's me." She quickly pulled it out. "It's my assistant." Remembering there was a proposal that night, she clicked to answer. "Hey, Marietta! What's up?"

"I'm so sorry, sweetie, but you need to come home. Your mother's been in an accident. She was hit by a car."

Her heart stopped. "Oh, my God!"

"She was awake enough to consent to surgery on her arm—which is broken—"

"She's in surgery!"

"Her arm was broken really bad. The doctors are telling us that she'll need a pin. Maybe two. She also has a concussion. They don't want you to worry, but they do want you here."

"Of course, I want to be there!" Fear trembled through her. Unlike Antonio who seemed to have people coming out of the woodwork, Riley only had her mom. If anything happened to her—

"I'll be on the next flight."

As soon as she clicked off the call, he said, "What's up?"

"My mom's been in an accident. She's in the hospital—having surgery. I have to go home."

He pulled out his phone. "My limo will take you back to your hotel, then to the airport."

Her imagination began forming all kinds of terrible scenarios. Her mother had gotten a call just like this one the night her father died. Not a kind nurse telling her that her significant other was dead, but a call to come to the hospital. In the twenty minutes it had taken to get there, her dad had died. If her mother's injuries were worse than they were telling her and she succumbed, Riley would be totally alone.

She took a quick breath, stopping her runaway imagination, and managed to hide her fears from Antonio. This wasn't his problem. It wasn't even really any of his business. Technically, they weren't even friends.

"Thanks. I have an open-ended ticket. Let's hope I can get a flight out today."

"I'm sure airlines have contingencies for emergencies."

Her airline did, but the next flight to New York wasn't for three hours. She booked it as she threw her things into her suitcases.

Antonio had waited for her in the limo. He wanted to ride with her to the airport, but she refused his offer. She was too nervous about her mom. She needed a clear head. Not the crazy brain of a woman pretending to be engaged to a guy she was so attracted to that a simple apology kiss had thrown her for a loop.

She had to get home to her mom.

During the two-hour wait for a flight, she prepared herself to see her mother hurt, broken. Italy was seven hours ahead. The flight took seven hours. They had taken off at three o'clock, so she landed in New York almost the same time that she'd left Italy.

Another hour was spent getting from the airport to the hospital. In the elevator to her mom's room, she glanced down to see Antonio's engagement ring. She hadn't been in Florence long enough to get it taken off—

It didn't matter.

Now that Antonio knew it had to be cut off, she could have the ring removed herself and find a courier service that could deliver it to him in Italy.

Technically, their relationship was over.

They'd never see each other again.

The feeling that she missed out on something good with him shuffled through her. She tried to soothe her disappointment with the knowledge that anything she'd had with him wouldn't be permanent. But that gave her small comfort. Meeting him, getting involved with him, had been a once-in-a-lifetime opportunity. A gorgeous Italian billionaire wanted her to pretend to be his fiancée. She'd all but swooned every time he touched her.

She laughed as the elevator doors opened.

It was a miracle she'd kept her wits about her.

She checked in at the nurses' station and they directed her to her mother's room.

She walked in to find two of her mom's employees. Jane Fineman, her mom's assistant and Pete Williams, her second in command.

Pete walked over and hugged her. "She's fine."

"And she can speak for herself," her mother mumbled from the bed.

"Surgery took a few hours," Pete continued. "But apparently, it's pretty routine stuff. She handled it like a champ."

Riley walked to the bed and hugged her mother as well as she could, given the IV and dressing on her arm. "You scared me to death."

"Hey, I didn't ask to get hit by a car at three o'clock in the morning."

"What were you doing out at three o'clock in the morning!"

"The doctor I was wining and dining likes clubs."

"You went clubbing!"

Riley's mom turned to Pete. "If she's going to be a buzz kill, she needs to leave."

Pete laughed. "Pain meds are making her silly."

Riley sighed. "You guys can go home."

"You all can go home. I would like to get some sleep."

With that, Juliette drifted off and Jane faced Riley. "We really should go. There are schedules to be made, employee problems to handle. Without your mom, everything falls to me and Pete."

Plus, if they'd been the people called by the hospital, they'd likely been here since four or five o'clock in the morning.

"Yes! Go!" Riley said.

Jane gathered her purse and Pete hugged Riley one more time before they left. Riley's mom slept soundly.

Riley glanced around. With everyone gone, the room was silent. She wished she'd bought a magazine or book from the newsstand at the airport, then remembered she had her phone. She found a word game and started playing. If she didn't keep her mind busy, she'd worry about her mom or think about Antonio and wonder if she'd made a mistake by not giving in to their chemistry. She didn't want to think about either of those. Too much had happened in a few short days. Including her mother's accident. Her brain needed a rest.

But thoughts of her time in Italy floated to her mind as she played the mindless game. Being with Antonio and his father and grandmother and being in a quiet hospital room with her mom right now, really brought home how alone she was. If that accident had killed her mom, she would have had no one.

No one.

It wasn't like she hadn't thought of that before. But her mom was only fifty. And she was strong.

A little bulldozer. Riley hadn't even considered that she could have an accident. Still, she knew, deep down, that having only her mom as family was what lured her to want a committed relationship. Not the idea of being in love—but the idea of having a family. The kind of family her friends had had when she was in grade school.

Parents, three kids and a dog—or cat. Crazy-busy breakfasts. Outings on weekends. Soccer games. A minivan. Lots to do besides reading in her condo when she didn't have work.

Even as she thought that, GiGi's feelings about Antonio getting married suddenly crystalized. Antonio's grandmother didn't want great-grandkids. Not that she wouldn't love great-grandkids, but her real motivation was that she did not want her only grandson to be alone. His grandfather was gone. GiGi herself was sick. And Antonio's dad was at least as old as Riley's mom. He had a mom, but he didn't speak much of her. He'd said she was an alcoholic, which brought its own problems, including illnesses.

In the blink of an eye, Antonio could be as alone as she was.

The idea amazed her. She'd thought he had people coming out of the woodwork, but just like her people, they were friends, coworkers, not family.

Neither one of them had much family to speak of.

And the people they did have were getting older.

She wondered if he ever thought about that, but decided it was none of her business. Undoubtedly, he thought having friends and coworkers and lovers was enough people in his life. And she supposed it was. Some friends were better than family.

Except Antonio had experienced having a family. She hadn't. She remembered times with her dad, but the memories were fleeting. Antonio knew what it was like to be surrounded by love, to be part of something, to always have Christmas dinner and summer vacations.

That's what made them different. It was why she wanted something he didn't even consider. His loving upbringing had satisfied a need Riley still had.

Close to eight o'clock that night, just when her phone battery was about to die, Marietta arrived.

She hugged Riley. "How is she?"

"She was well enough to give me a hard time when I got here. Then she immediately fell asleep. She's been asleep ever since."

Marietta nodded. "Has the doctor been in?"

"The nurse told me he had another emergency surgery, but he'd be in before he left the hospital for the day." She paused, then realized why Marietta hadn't arrived until almost eight.

"Did tonight's proposal go well?"

Marietta smiled broadly. "I wondered when you'd ask."

Riley glanced at her mom. "I guess we now know what it takes for me to forget about work."

Marietta patted her hand. "She's going to be fine."

"Eventually. She didn't just break her arm. She also has a concussion. I have to be patient."

"Hospital is the best place for her right now."

Riley sighed. "I guess."

"I know!" Marietta said, then she grinned. "And the proposal was as smooth as pudding."

Riley finally noticed how bright her assistant's eyes were. "You had fun doing it!"

"I did! Now I see why you're so obsessed with work. It was so much fun! They were so happy. It was pure magic."

Riley laughed. "It always is." Antonio's proposal to her popped into her head and sadness filled her. Maybe it was all the emotion of the day, but it seemed a shame that something that looked so good was fake.

Plus, she missed him. She missed a guy she'd met a few days ago. How could she miss him? Why was she even thinking about him? He was out of her life. Poof. Never to be seen again.

Marietta left to get coffee and a sandwich from a nearby vendor. She hadn't been gone two minutes before the tall, balding doctor wearing scrubs came in and told Riley that her mom would be going home the next day, or the day after if there was a complication.

"But I don't believe there will be. The surgery was textbook. We'll keep her here tonight and if she's well enough, then tomorrow she can go home. It will all depend on her concussion status."

"Thank you, Doctor."

"You should go home and get some sleep too. I heard you were in Italy."

"I was."

"This must have been a long day for you."

"Yes." Thirty-six hours already. And she still wasn't home.

"Well, go. We'll talk in the morning."

By the time Marietta returned, Riley was ready to leave. Now that her adrenaline was wearing off, she could have dropped where she stood.

They took a cab. Marietta had the driver let Riley off at her condo building first. The doorman gave her a goofy grin as he opened the door to the lobby for her.

"Evening, Miss Morgan."

"Evening, Oscar."

As she entered the lobby, a man rose from one of the convenience sofas. She stopped. Her mouth dropped open. "Antonio?"

"My grandmother went nuts when she heard that your mother had been in an accident, and she shooed me across the ocean to be with my fiancée."

So tired that she was giddy, that struck Riley as hysterically funny, and she laughed. "The more you try to be a make-believe fiancé, the more your GiGi shoves you into the role for real."

"I do not think it's funny."

"Oh, you should be up for thirty-six hours. *Everything's* funny."

He caught her arm and directed her to the elevator. "Let's get you to your condo."

She clung to his arm. "Good idea."

CHAPTER SEVEN

THE ELEVATOR DOOR opened as soon as he hit the button. They rode in silence to her floor, then walked to the last door on the right, which she unlocked.

Following her, he stepped inside the condo, looking around with approval at the white stacked stone fireplace, dark hardwood floors, and white area rug that matched the white sofa and chair with multicolored print throw pillows.

"Wow. Somebody must be making good money."

She tossed her purse to the kitchen island of the open-concept space. "This condo was my reward the first year my company reached a two-million-dollar profit."

"Two million dollars for planning proposals?"

"Have you seen *your* invoice?"

He laughed. But he watched her closely. She was so tired that her arms moved like noodles.

"Plus, I believed I deserved a nice home for all my hard work."

He wondered if a home was the first thing she'd bought because her father's family kicked her and her mom out of the condo they were living in when he died. But he didn't mention that. She hadn't argued about him coming to her condo with her, and though he could get a hotel room, his GiGi was right. She needed him and he had the relentless sense that he should be taking care of her.

"Come on. Let's get you to bed."

She leaned in and whispered, "I thought you'd never ask."

He snorted. "In the morning, you're going to wish you hadn't said that."

"Why? Are you going to take advantage of me?"

"I told you. I don't have to take advantage of women. I'm assuming this condo has two bedrooms?"

She pouted. "It does."

He shook his head as he helped her down the hall. She pointed at a door. "That's the spare room."

He nodded. "Okay. That'll be my room."

They walked to the second door. "And this will be my room."

"Are you good to shower by yourself?"

Her big green eyes grew serious. "Honestly, I'm so tired that I'm just going to face-plant on the bed."

He laughed. "How about if I come in with you and turn down the covers while you take off your shoes."

"Okay."

Her agreement was so subdued that he missed silly Riley, but he knew her getting back to normal was for the best. As she kicked off her shoes, he pulled down the comforter, then the sheet and plumped the pillow.

"There."

She walked over to him, stood on her tiptoes and kissed him. "Thank you."

The spontaneity of it took him by surprise and he blinked. He'd kissed her and she'd kissed him back, but she'd never kissed him first. So innocently. So honestly. The pleasure of it rode his blood in the oddest way. Not as arousal, as he would have expected. But as happiness.

She liked him.

That was what all her silliness had been about. She'd been too tired to pretend indifference.

A smile formed before he could stop it.

She climbed into bed, pulled the covers to her chin and closed her eyes.

He walked to the door, said, "Good night," then left her room, shutting the door behind him.

In her kitchen, he found nothing to eat. All the cupboards were bare, as if they'd just been installed by the contractor. He opened the refrigerator. Though there was no food, there was a nice assortment of beer.

He frowned. Unless she'd just had a party and this was leftover beer, there might be a man in her life. His chest tightened at the possibility. Then he remembered their conversation in her hotel room the night before. Good God! Had it only been one night ago? It felt like forever. Like he'd known her forever and that conversation was in their distant past.

If there had been a man in her life, she would have told him when he was ragging on her about looking for real love.

He still felt bad about that, even though he'd apologized. But he'd apologized with a spontaneous kiss, that—just like the easy kiss she'd given him that night—told him he liked her.

Still a little flummoxed over the way she'd kissed him, he should get a hotel, lie to his GiGi and make up stories about her mother being fine, but that didn't sit right. He did not want to go through another bout of feeling guilty over her. He would stay at least one day to make sure Riley and her mother really were okay. And if he was staying, the cupboards would not be bare.

Not wanting to dig too deeply into that, he opened drawers looking for takeout menus and found several. He ordered Chinese, then went to the lobby to wait for it and also to have a chat with Oscar.

As soon as he saw him, Oscar straightened. "Mr. Salvaggio? Leaving?"

"No. I ordered Chinese. I thought I'd come down and wait for it."

"I could have brought it up!"

"I actually wanted to ask you where a person gets groceries around here."

Oscar said, "Lots of people order things online. You know, from the usual places. But there's a grocery around the corner."

"If I order online, will it come to you?"

He nodded.

"Riley's mom had an accident and we'll be at the hospital tomorrow." He pulled a few bills out of his wallet. "If you could take a delivery that would be great."

Oscar raised his hands. "You don't have to pay me. That's a service of the building."

"Consider it a thank you."

Taking the money, Oscar nodded. "I'll handle it personally."

Antonio's Chinese food came, and he returned to the condo. After putting his dinner on a plate, he took a seat at the big kitchen island and started scrolling on his phone. He found two sites with one-day delivery, ordered food for breakfast and dinner as he ate. Even if it didn't come until tomorrow afternoon, Riley would have food for breakfast and dinner the following day.

After tidying the kitchen, he went into the living room where he turned on the big screen TV. He should have felt uncomfortable in her house, but the easy way she'd kissed him matched the feeling of ease he had in her home.

It was a bit disconcerting.

But it also felt right. She'd kissed him. He'd helped her into bed and ordered food for the next day. He couldn't remember the last time simple things had given him such pleasure.

Because he liked her too. He wasn't merely attracted to her. He liked her. Comfortable in her living room, he couldn't deny that that meant something. He might not want what she wanted but that didn't have to mean they couldn't have *something*. And more than a friendship. Something real. Something fun.

Maybe his grandmother sending him to Manhattan was a second chance of a sort? They might not be meant to be together forever, but he couldn't shake the feeling they should have a romance. A happy and passionate affair. He knew she didn't want that. But the sense that they were made for *something* wouldn't leave him.

He went to bed not sure of anything, except that she had considered sleeping with him. She might have been so tired she was punch drunk, but sometimes when people were vulnerable the truth came out.

She'd definitely thought about sleeping with him.

He couldn't stop another smile because for the first time since he'd met her, he wasn't off balance.

Riley woke the next morning in the clothes she'd had on the day before. She gasped and jumped out of bed. Now, her sheets were covered in airplane germs!

Wasting no time, she walked to the hall linen closet and when she turned away from getting new linens, she saw her guest room door was closed.

Her eyes widened. She'd forgotten Antonio!

She raced into her room, changed her sheets, tossed the airport germ sheets into the laundry, then she showered and dressed for the day. She was *not* dressing special for him. It was Saturday. She had to go to the hospital to take care of everything with her mom. Jeans. A summer-weight sweater. Comfortable tennis shoes. That was it.

She glanced at her face in the mirror and winced.

All right. So, she would put on makeup. No respectable single woman in Manhattan went out without makeup. Traveling so much had given her black eyes and saggy cheeks. Both needed a boost. A little lip gloss wouldn't hurt either.

Satisfied, she took a long breath before she opened her bedroom door and swore she smelled coffee. The scent increased as she walked into the common area of the house. Antonio stood in front of the big island.

"Good morning!"

She drank in the sight of him. She'd missed him and he'd appeared in her condo building as if by magic. Nothing would come of this relationship, but she was not going to be stuffy about him being here. Sure, his GiGi had sent him, but he'd come. If she remembered the night before correctly, he had helped her as his GiGi had said he should.

For once, she would take his presence at face value and not overthink things.

"Good morning." She ambled to the cupboard, got a mug and made herself a cup of coffee in the one-cup coffeemaker. "Did you sleep well?"

"Yes. Like you, I'd been up over twenty-four hours."

She winced and took a seat at the center island. "I might have handled it more poorly than you did."

"Your mother had been hurt. You were upset. You had a right to be off your game. How is she by the way?"

"She might be released this morning."

"Oh."

"I'll probably have her stay here with me for a few days."

"If that's a polite way of telling me that my room will be spoken for tonight. I get the hint. Plus, that's a good excuse for me to give my GiGi…that with your mom here I'd be in the way."

Disappointment tumbled through her. She hadn't meant to kick him out. It seemed she was always doing that. Just when things could be normal between them, she did or said something that made her sound less than hospitable.

She tried to fix it. "Or maybe you could handle some business here? You know, get a hotel and do some work?"

"GiGi would like it if I spent a few days here. And my last trip was unexpectedly cut short."

He glanced at her hand.

She looked down at the ring too. "Maybe we could find a jeweler?"

He cleared his throat. "Maybe."

She'd been so preoccupied with joy that he was here, she hadn't noticed he wore a white T-shirt and pajama pants. The intimacy of it almost stopped her breathing.

She now knew what he slept in.

And he knew she'd slept in her clothes.

He sat beside her.

She wanted nothing more than to take advantage of having him here with her, to talk and laugh the way they had when she'd planned his proposal, or at his family's vineyard, but she couldn't think of anything clever to say.

She sipped her coffee. This was ridiculous. Nothing felt right, the way it had in Italy, and she had a mother to attend to. She shouldn't be thinking about Antonio and trying to make something happen between them.

She slid off her stool, taking her coffee with her. "I have to get to the hospital. Doctors get there early, you know. I don't want to miss him and have to wait until night rounds to talk to him."

"Unless your mom is released today."

"I still need to talk to him. My mom's a nurse. She's going to try to buffalo me into believing she's better than she is."

He laughed.

"I need to ask all my questions at the source." Spotting her purse on the counter where she'd left it the night before, she grabbed it and headed for the door.

"Good-bye."

She turned. Realizing she looked like she was giving him the bum's rush again, she softened her tone and said, "Good-bye. Thanks for your help last night."

His eyes shifted, sparked with something so male she nearly lost her breath. "You're welcome."

She raced out of her condo, needing to get away from all that sincerity and those beautiful dark eyes. Things might not be as easy between them as they had been in Italy, but he was still gorgeous.

And...

Had she asked him if he was taking her to bed the night before?

She groaned. She had. The memory came back vividly.

But they were in a fake relationship. The day before, she'd gotten herself to accept that. This morning, if she'd been a little less in control, she

could have fallen back in that trap again of thinking something was happening between them.

It wasn't.

She wouldn't let herself think it was.

Antonio stared at the door. He'd seen the longing
glances she'd given him, but she'd raced out, as if
she couldn't get away from him fast enough. Of
course, she was worried about her mother, and
he didn't blame her.

He showered and was about to put on a clean
shirt and trousers when it hit him that this was
Saturday.

Only the most diligent would be working.
Without the crises that had brought him to New
York the weekend before, he would not work on
a weekend.

He sighed, shifted from trousers and a dress
shirt to jeans and a T-shirt, then he glanced around
with another sigh. He didn't have anywhere he
needed to be. But he also didn't feel like hanging
out in Riley's condo or taking a walk in the park.

She hadn't told him much about her mother's
accident or condition, except that she might be
released that day, and the guest room would be
needed for her. She'd been so uncomfortable that
morning that he'd known better than to ask. But
GiGi would ask. He needed more info.

He used his phone to search the internet and
found her company's website, along with the

phone numbers for her and her assistant. Not wanting to interrupt Riley when she was with her mom, he dialed her assistant.

An hour later, his limo let him off in front of the main entrance to the hospital. He took the elevator to her floor and strode to her room.

Riley bounced out of her chair. "Antonio?"

He walked in, hugged her and gave her a proper kiss, for the benefit of the pretty blonde woman lying in the bed, in case she wasn't in on the fact that their engagement was fake. Having caught her off guard, the kiss was equal parts passion and sweetness, and the idea that this might be a second chance for them again popped into his brain.

She pulled back, dazed. "What are you doing here?"

He displayed the flowers he'd brought. "First, these are for your mother."

The blonde in the bed smiled weakly. "So, you're Antonio."

Riley seemed to come back to life. "Antonio, this is my mother, Juliette Morgan. Mom, this is Antonio Salvaggio... I told you about him."

Her mom closed her eyes. "Yes, you did. It's nice to meet you, Antonio. Thank you for the flowers." Then she took a breath and it seemed she fell asleep.

"She's been in and out like that all morning. The doctor said it's nothing to worry about. All part of recovering from the trauma of being hit by a car." She caught his gaze. "You didn't have to come here."

"Actually, I need some solid facts for my grandmother. I know she's worried, so I thought a real visit was in order."

"Okay—" She glanced at her mother. "As you can see, she's sleeping a lot and the doctor recommended she stay another day."

"She's staying another day?" He shifted his gaze to Riley's. "Meaning, the extra room in your condo will be open again tonight."

CHAPTER EIGHT

RILEY STARED INTO Antonio's eyes and knew exactly what he was telling her. With her mom not coming home with her that night, he could sleep there.

Marietta came racing into the room. "Oh, I see you're here!" she said to Antonio.

He chuckled. For a billionaire, he had an uncanny way of looking perfectly comfortable even in the oddest situations.

"Yes. You must be Marietta."

"We sort of met the day you planned your proposal to Riley."

"Yes. We did. You make great coffee."

She blushed. "I wish I could take credit for it, but Riley had everything set up for you. I just poured it." She faced Riley. "Could I have a minute with you in the hall?"

Riley's heart stopped. "Why? What happened with yesterday's proposal?"

"We should talk about it in the hall."

Riley raced out behind Marietta and said, "Give it to me straight. Whatever went wrong, we can fix it."

"Nothing went wrong. I told you last night that it was perfect, but you were so tired you probably forgot. I was hoping to beat your Italian god to the hospital so I could warn you he was coming. He called and asked for the hospital your mom was in, and I couldn't think of a good reason not to tell him…since he is your fiancé."

Riley groaned. "Fake fiancé."

"I know but it just felt wrong not telling him." She peeked into Juliette's hospital room. "He's such a nice guy."

He was a nice guy. Considerate and gorgeous. Which is exactly what made him so tempting. Until she remembered he was like her other boyfriends. He wasn't somebody who would settle down. Ever. Her mom's accident reminded her that she was alone—that she needed things a man like Antonio couldn't give her. No matter how happy she'd been to see him, she needed to keep her distance.

"He's a great guy, but we're really not engaged. Not a couple. Nothing at all between us."

Marietta looked at Riley again. "Really? Nothing?"

She winced. "Well, not *nothing* nothing. I'm not dead. The guy is gorgeous. And so suave." She almost sighed. "Seriously, mouth-watering sexy."

Marietta laughed. "So, what's the problem? Why aren't you enjoying this?"

Not wanting to admit her weird feelings, Riley gave the obvious excuse. "He's a client."

"No. He's not. His proposal is over."

"Were it not for this stupid ring," she said, waving it at Marietta. "This whole mess would be over. Instead, he's here when he shouldn't be."

"Really?"

"Yes. He's only here because his grandmother told him he should be with his fiancée when her mother is in the hospital."

Marietta gave her the strangest look. "Do you think he's only here because his grandmother sent him?"

She combed her fingers through her hair. His grandmother might have told him to come, but he hadn't needed to actually visit the hospital. "I don't know."

"He likes you. I could hear it in his voice."

"He also doesn't believe in love."

"So, you've talked about it?"

"Yes, when we were deciding we were not letting anything happen between us."

"You talked about *that* too?"

She sighed. "Look, don't go making a bigger deal out of this than it needs to be."

"I'm not making it a big deal. You are. The guy is sexy, good looking. He's also considerate. Under that suave billionaire persona there seems to be a great guy. He came to check on your mother. Give him a chance."

"No. We want two different things."

"Okay. How about this? You've been so stressed lately, why not—you know."

Her face scrunched. "No. I do not know."

"Why not have a little fling?"

She gaped at Marietta. "Because nothing can come of it!"

"Can't you just, for once, have some fun?"

"I need more in my life than fun—"

"You know what? You do need more in your life and someday you'll probably get it. You'll find a guy who wants forever with you. But that doesn't mean you have to mourn until you find him or he finds you. In fact, maybe a little fun would make you happy enough that you'd see other opportunities. Maybe even see the right guy."

She'd never looked at it like that before. Had she been so busy, so intense, that she'd actually missed opportunities?

"Lots of guys have looked at you like they might be interested, but you have this way of being all business with everyone."

"Probably because most of the men I deal with come to me wanting me to plan their marriage proposal."

"Yeah, but a lot of those guys have had friends or cousins. You don't even see them, do you?"

"You're talking about people who come to watch the proposals?"

"Yes."

She blinked. Many people came to proposals. Parents. Grandparents. Friends of both the bride and groom. That's what made the more elaborate events fun. But she never scouted the crowd looking for Prince Charming. She never glanced at the crowd at all. She was too busy working.

Always working.

"I do have a job to do—"

"Yeah." Marietta winced. "But sometimes you're so intense that I think people are afraid to approach you."

She gasped. "I scare people off?"

"Maybe scaring people off is a bit dramatic. It's more like guys take one look at you and know you're so busy, so intense, that there's no point in approaching you."

She blinked. "Oh."

"Oh, honey. I don't mean to insult you. But you never have any fun. And I want you to have fun. You're the nicest, most wonderful person I know. You're so good to your employees we become your friends. But you're not very kind to yourself."

Shell-shocked, Riley said, "Okay. I can see that might be true."

Marietta glanced at her watch. "I've gotta run. Lots of stuff to do today. But think about what I said."

Riley returned to her mother's room, her head down, still gobsmacked. Antonio sat on the visitor's chair, reading his phone.

"Anything interesting on that phone?"

"Just a message that the groceries I ordered for you last night have been delivered."

"You ordered groceries for me?"

"You had no food. With your mother in the hospital, I thought it wiser not to have to go to a restaurant for breakfast...or to grab a donut."

Weird feelings bubbled up. According to her assistant, she never noticed guys who might be interested in her. Antonio had spent the night with her in her apartment, and he'd bought her food. Because his grandmother had shipped him to New York to be with her or because he was a genuinely good guy?

"You're right. I probably wouldn't have stopped for more than a cup of coffee."

"Under stress like this, you need real food and it's now in your building."

The kindness of the gesture almost overwhelmed her, but she couldn't stop thinking of what Marietta had said. Was she intense? So driven she never noticed other people?

No. Caring for other people was her job. What Marietta had said was she never was kind to herself. And that she never had any fun.

Which was true. A good book was as close as she got to a good time.

"Oscar texted that he'll run the order up to your apartment."

Confusion tightened her chest. "Oscar texted you?"

He tucked his phone into his jacket pocket. "Yes."

"He normally doesn't get that friendly."

He shrugged. "What can I say? People like me."

She winced. "Meaning, I'm the first person you don't get along with."

"You and I were getting along just fine until we got engaged."

She snickered. "That was all your idea."

He motioned to the ring on her finger, suddenly serious. "If we can leave your mom, we can probably find a jeweler and have that removed."

She glanced down at it, "It would be a good idea, but I don't feel right leaving today. The doctor's not supposed to check in until this afternoon." She glanced at her sleeping mom.

He rose from his chair, walked over and hugged her. "Okay. I understand."

It felt so wonderful to be hugged by him that she could have wept. But she had no idea why. Her mother was going to be fine. Still, he had thought she needed a hug, and he gave her one.

Antonio said, "I'll see you at home."

She sniffed a laugh at the way he'd said *at home*. Her home, but he was clearly comfortable there.

"I'll make dinner."

A hug was one thing. Making her dinner was

special. No one ever did things like that for her. She was always the one doing things for other people.

She pulled out of his hug. "Really?"

"Sure."

She studied his face, so confused about him she didn't know what to think. "I just don't picture billionaires cooking."

"We're people too. We have likes and dislikes and twenty-four hours to fill every day."

"I thought you had yachts for that."

He snorted. "Seriously? I might not have to work six days a week, but I like to use my brain and my talents."

"Cooking is one of those talents?"

"It's a form of creativity."

"It is."

They smiled at each other. The sense of connection filled her again, except this time it wasn't an ethereal whisper of fate. It was tangible. The intuition that something was happening between them wasn't her imagination. They liked each other and it was blissfully wonderful.

And spectacularly wrong. With all the realizations she had made because of her mom being in the hospital, her feelings were raw, and she was needy. She could fall in love with him so easily.

Or would she?

She knew going in that this relationship would end. And she was a pretty smart cookie. If she looked at this as two people who liked each other, enjoying the limited time they had together, she could hold her feelings in check.

Plus…

What if Marietta was right? What if she was so intent on doing her job that she missed the cues that someone was interested in her? Worse, what if she really was scaring people off—

What if she *did* need a fling with an Italian billionaire to get back her sense of fun?

The talk with the doctor went exactly as she'd thought. Her mom's condition had not improved in the twelve hours since she'd seen him. She would be spending at least another night.

When visiting hours were over, she texted Antonio and told him she was about to get a cab. He told her he'd already sent his limo for her.

The happy sensation filled her again—the knowledge that Antonio was someone special. Not just a billionaire with a great family and vineyard so gorgeous it felt like heaven. But a considerate person.

Oscar grinned at her as she entered her building lobby. "Evening, Riley."

"Evening, Oscar."

"Antonio's upstairs."

"Yes. He texted me."

"Great guy."

"I know."

She entered the elevator. She did know. The man loved his grandmother enough to fake a proposal. He was helping her find venues for her work in Italy. Now, while her mother was in the hospital, he was here with her for support.

She stepped into her condo and smelled the crisp scent of marinara sauce.

He glanced up from the pot he was stirring. "How did things go?"

She rolled her shoulders, not really tired, more like stiff from stress. "You mean with the doctor?"

"Yes."

"He hadn't changed his mind about Mom staying another day."

He nodded, then held out a spoon of red sauce for her to taste. "Try this."

She gingerly took a sip. "Oh." She groaned with pleasure. "That's delicious."

"I'm guessing you didn't eat lunch."

"You guess right."

"Go. Take a quick shower and put on something comfortable. The spaghetti needs eight minutes. I'll wait two before I put it in water, giving you ten minutes."

She laughed and raced back to her room, so eager for a shower she could have kissed him. Removing her clothes, she realized again how easily she thought about kissing him. She paused, thinking that through. Though anything they had would be a fling, it wouldn't be casual or spur of the moment. It would be wonderful, memorable.

Which was exactly what was missing from her life. Something wonderful. Something memorable. Something that marked the end of old, intense, all-business Riley and the beginning of the Riley who would be approachable.

And he stood in her kitchen right now, making her dinner.

Her shower took two minutes, choosing clothes and applying just enough makeup that she didn't look like a ghost took the rest of the time.

She ambled to the stove wearing yoga pants and a cute top, not wanting to appear to have dressed up for him, but also looking enticing enough that she could flirt. Maybe even make a pass at him.

The stove timer went off.

"You just made it. Not a second to spare."

She smiled. "It's the best way to run a business. You can't ever be late…but you also can't appear too eager."

He laughed. "That's true about a lot of things." Wearing her seldom used oven mitts because she didn't have potholders, he removed the pan of pasta from the stove and dumped it into a colander that she didn't even know she had. Then he put the spaghetti on two plates. "I'll let you pour your own sauce. The pasta can cool a bit while we eat our salads."

He carried them to the table. She followed him

and saw that the meatballs and sauce were already there. Two plates of salad sat in front of two chairs, and he'd decorated her little table with candles, along with her good silver and the linen napkins that her mom had bought her when she purchased the condo. There was also a bottle of wine. He must have explored the neighborhood before he started cooking.

"This is lovely."

"In Italy, we call this casual."

She laughed as she sat.

He sat too. "So, you said your mom needs time?"

"At least one more day. I reminded the doctor that she runs a home nursing agency, and she employs about a hundred nurses who could care for her, and he said he'll take that into consideration when deciding when she can come home."

"Do you think bringing her home is wise?"

"I think when she finally wakes up for more than an hour at a time, she's going to demand she be allowed to go home."

"Staying up for more than an hour at a time will probably mean she's *ready* to go home."

"That's a good way to look at it."

She dug into her salad.

"And you are fine?"

"Actually, I'm pretty good. Sitting in her room for two days forced me to slow down." She glanced over at him. "Think about things."

He studied her for a second. "You've never done that?"

"I haven't had a vacation in six years. Lots of proposals happen on weekends. When I get home, I take a shower, read a book and think about what's on the schedule for the week to come."

He pointed his fork at her. "If you were in Italy, I'd make you slow down. Enjoy the scenery."

"I enjoyed your GiGi...and the tour of your beautiful vineyard."

"There is so much more to see."

She almost told him that when she returned to Italy to visit the vendors Geoffrey had found for her, she would take him up on that offer. But what they had wasn't about the future. It was an in-the-moment thing. Which was the best way to enjoy it. No promises. No plans. Just let whatever happened happen. That way, no one got hurt.

"Tell me a little bit about you."

His head tilted as if the question confused him. "You've met my family. Seen my office."

"Yeah. But I'd like to hear something no one else knows."

He laughed. "Really?"

"Sure."

"Something silly?"

"No. Something that tells me about who you are."

He took a breath. "Something that tells you about who I am?" He picked up her salad plate, then his and carried them to the kitchen. When he returned, he handed her a plate of pasta, then offered her the bowl of sauce.

"We're so different," she said, explaining her reasoning when it seemed like he might not share. "I'm just trying to get to know you."

"Okay." He thought for a second. "When I was fifteen, I tried to run away to Norway."

Knowing that was where his mother lived, she perked up. "Really?"

"Yes. My father had disciplined me for something, and I decided my mom would be a lot easier on me and I was going to live with her. I thought life with her would be wonderful. She was alone. She always said she missed me. I saw myself moving in with her and nothing but happiness."

She leaned in, eager for the chance to know more about him. "What happened?"

He took a breath. "It's almost a two-day train ride to Norway because there's no direct route. And don't even get me started on the ferry."

"You were bored?"

He snorted. "No. By the time I got there my father was already there. He had taken a plane."

"That's funny!" She peered at him. "Why aren't you laughing?"

He set down his fork, sighed. "That was the day, I met my real mom."

She frowned. "Oh."

"Thinking my mom and I needed some private

time, my father left us alone to talk things out."
He shook his head. "The two hours I spent with
her were…the worst of my life."

"Showing you that living with your mom wasn't
a better option than your dad?"

"It was more than that." He took a breath, as
if thinking through his answer and finally said,
"My mother was a train wreck. Drinking mostly."

Her mouth opened slightly but no sound came
out. He'd said she was an alcoholic, but obviously
that one word didn't convey the truth of the situation.

"When my father met her, she was a fun-loving
party girl. He adored her. They always had a great
time together. They married. She got pregnant and
he settled in, but she didn't. Very shortly after that
he realized she was drinking a lot. Not just when
they went out, or at dinner, but all day. Every day.
He soon recognized she was an alcoholic. When
they had the fight that ended their marriage, she
knew she was in trouble, but she didn't want to
get help. She liked herself. Her life…just the way
it was. She said she could manage her drinking
and my dad was just looking for a way to get rid
of her."

He shrugged. "She's my mother and I love her.
But the day I visited her, the minute my dad left,
she made a drink, then another, then another.
She's not managing anything."

"How long did your dad leave you with her?"

"Not even an hour and I suspect he spent the time right outside her apartment complex. That visit—as short as it was—explained a lot to me about my parents' divorce. Explained a lot about my mother. I thought—believed—she loved me and in her own way she did. But the daydream that she was lonely without me was nothing but wishful thinking."

Riley sat back. That visit with his mom might have shown him a lot of things, but it also explained his stance on marriage and love. His dad loved his mom, but that love died. Then his own marriage fell apart. And his relationship with his mother was nothing but wishful thinking.

It was no wonder he didn't believe love existed.

Still, his grandmother had shown him real love. So had his father. "Your dad seems like a nice guy."

"My father is a very smart man, whose only mistake was marrying my mother. He should have seen the obvious when they were dating and engaged. He didn't. He'll tell you that himself. He takes full responsibility."

She winced. "You and your dad have bad marriages in common."

Obviously trying to lighten the mood, he said, "And a love of casinos, good wine and a solid business deal."

"That's enough to make me think you're just like your father."

"I would say yes, but no man in his right mind admits that."

"Ah."

He took the sauce bowl from her. "Now, you tell me something about you… I think I'd like to hear about you and your mom. It seems like you two are also alike."

She winced. "We are. Although one of the things I realized today was that following in her footsteps and being such a bulldog about my company…the way she is about hers…might have made me—"

She stopped, unable to think of the word without embarrassing herself.

"Made you?"

"I'm not sure. Stern comes to mind."

He laughed.

"Formidable."

"I like that one."

She took a breath. "Unapproachable."

He stopped the sauce spoon two inches from his plate. "Unapproachable?" He shook his head. "No. Even frazzled from exhaustion the night I met you, you were lovely." He smiled. "Actually, I saw you before the proposal began and I couldn't take my eyes off you. You were focused. But even trying to blend into the background you were beautiful."

Her heart stuttered and tears of joy tried to form in her eyes, but she wouldn't let them. *This* was what having an affair with a suave Italian billionaire should be. Compliments that touch the heart. Easy conversation. Discussions about things like vineyards and villas. And delicious pasta.

"Thank you."

"Eat your spaghetti. We got off on a serious topic when tonight was supposed to be all about you resting." He pointed at her plate. "And getting some carbs in you."

She laughed. Her shoulders relaxed. He was perfect for an affair. A short, happy fling that would help her to stop being so serious. Especially now that she understood how he'd formed his beliefs about marriage. There was no chance he'd ever love again, so she wouldn't allow herself to fall for him. She'd keep her goals in mind. Her need to loosen up and take time to enjoy life so that—as Marietta had said—when the right guy came along, she'd actually see him. Not be so tense. Be ready and open.

All she had to do was figure out a way to seduce Antonio.

No ideas came as they ate, but she refused to push. She was supposed to be relaxed, comfortable, open. Not tense. Not trying to figure everything out.

When their spaghetti was gone, Antonio rose to clear the table. As he gathered the plates and silver, she picked up the bowl of marinara.

"I'll put this in the fridge."

He paused on his way to the dishwasher. "Are you going to eat it tomorrow?"

She frowned. "I don't know."

"Why don't you freeze it? Then someday when you're hungry and you pull it out for dinner, you'll think of me."

"That sounds nice." It did. Everything about him tonight was warm and fuzzy. After two glasses of wine, she was a bit warm and fuzzy herself.

She headed to the cupboard to find a storage container for the marinara just as he walked by on his way to the sink. He looked up at the same time that she looked over and they both jerked to a stop.

He smiled. She smiled. This was what she wanted them to be. Two people who knew each other and liked each other, gravitating toward more than friendship because of their attraction. Nothing strained. No confusion. Just letting something happen between them.

Once they cleared the table and cleaned the kitchen, they could watch TV together on the sofa and maybe, sitting close, their attraction would evolve naturally. No pushing. No fussing.

He motioned to the cupboard. His voice was deep and sexy when he said, "You go ahead."

"I'm just getting a bowl for the marinara."

He smiled again. His dark eyes glittered with desire.

Her skin felt like it caught fire. When he'd kissed her, she'd melted. She couldn't imagine how intense making love would be. But she wanted it.

She retrieved a container that she could freeze and walked over to the center island, giving him space to finish stacking dishes in the dishwasher. Her kitchen wasn't small but this thing that hummed between them made even the biggest space seem tiny, the innocent nearness of their bodies powerful.

She drew in a long breath. Anticipation scared her silly, even as it made her breathless. He finished the dishes. She slid the bowl of marinara into the freezer. She set it on a shelf and closed the door, but a realization struck her.

He'd asked if she would be eating the sauce the next day. As if he wouldn't be there. Was he going home? Tonight?

She told herself she was being silly, overthinking things. He would tell her if he was planning to go home. Her nerves were getting the better of her.

She followed him to the sofa, knowing if something was going to happen it would be on the sofa with them sitting close.

He picked up the remote but tossed it down again.

"You know what? You're tired and I have some calls to make."

She struggled not to gape at him. He was going to ignore this sizzle! She almost couldn't believe it—

Except she'd spent most of their relationship giving him negative signals. Somehow, she needed to turn that around.

"I'm not tired." She yawned. Damn it! Where the hell had that come from?

He laughed. "You are tired." With a wave of his hand, he directed her to follow him. "Come on. Let me walk you to your room."

She sighed internally. Marietta was right. She wasn't any good at this and she did need a fling to get her groove back.

"That's okay. I know the way."

"Agreed. But maybe I'd like to steal a kiss."

Her breath stalled. It seemed she'd read his suggestion that she go to bed all wrong. Saying she was tired might have been his way of getting them back to her bedroom?

He caught her hand, and they walked down the short hall. When they got to her door, he said, "Good night."

She smiled. This was sweet and romantic, but she was ready for more. "Good night."

He dipped his head to kiss her, and she slid her hands up his shirt front to his shoulders. She totally relaxed, let herself sink into the kiss. The feeling of his lips on hers. The solidness of his shoulders. The way their bodies brushed just enough to tempt and tease her. Every fiber of her being woke up. Her breath shivered into her lungs.

He pulled away suddenly. "This is awful."

She blinked. "Kissing me is awful?"

He groaned. "No. Having to stop is awful!"

She stepped close again. The time for signals and hints was over. She needed to be direct and honest. "You don't have to stop."

He held her gaze. "Yes, I do. You're coming down from the adrenaline of flying across an ocean to be with your mother, and two days of sitting at the hospital, worrying. You're not think-ing straight."

"I'm pretty sure I've thought this through com-pletely and I know what I'm doing."

"You're ready for an affair?"

She held his gaze. "Yes. I realized I've been all about work these past years and I'm in need of a real life. This," she motioned from herself to him and back to herself again, "the off-the-charts thing between us, is too tempting to be resisted. In fact, I'm pretty sure it's not supposed to be resisted."

"I agree. But—" He shook his head. "You thought it through while your emotions were all garbled." He took a breath and looked at the ceiling. "Making love is supposed to be wonder-ful. Sweet. Sexy. And mutually fun. Your whole world's been tossed up in the air the past few days. Give your emotions a chance to settle down."

Her chest tightened. Was that what these new feelings were? Her heightened emotions looking for release? She didn't know whether to be angry with herself or embarrassed.

Just when embarrassed would have won, he caught her elbows, pulled her to him and kissed her so sweetly she almost swooned. For a guy who didn't believe in love or the permanency of that emotion, he conveyed more to her in a slow romantic kiss than anybody ever had.

He pulled back. "Good night." With a flip of his wrist, he opened her bedroom door, then shifted to the right, giving her enough space to walk past him.

When she was inside her room, he closed the door and she stood frozen. Longing rippled through her. Kissing him always stirred up her hormones but tonight had been about more. She'd never felt closer to another human being than she had to him. What he'd told her about his mom, his parents, was the kind of thing you only revealed when you trusted someone.

He trusted her.

She liked him. And he liked her. The fact that he'd turned her down actually endeared him to her a little bit more.

She slid into pajamas and then into bed. She wasn't sure what would happen in the morning, but a warm feeling filled her heart. She fell asleep almost immediately, proving him right. She had been tired.

When she woke, she showered and dressed in jeans and a sleeveless blouse. After putting on a comfortable pair of sandals, she left her room and headed toward the kitchen. The door to the spare bedroom was open. The lights were off. But she saw the dim glow from the kitchen and smelled fresh coffee.

She pulled in a breath, straightened her shoulders and walked up the corridor, not quite sure what she was expecting when she stepped up to the center island.

Antonio leaned against it, reading his phone. Obviously having heard her enter, he looked up and smiled. "If I'd known you were waking so early, I would have made you a cup of coffee."

Her heart liquefied. He had no idea what a wonderful person he was.

"I can do it." She ambled to the cupboard and pulled out a mug.

Memories of the way he'd kissed her the night before drifted through her brain. The sweetness of it weakened her knees. Anticipation stole through her. She wasn't tired now. He would know that. If he kissed her again, this would be it. They would sleep together.

"I have to go back to Italy today."

Well, that wasn't what she'd been expecting. She stopped halfway to the coffeemaker. Then she remembered his suggestion that she freeze the marinara sauce and disappointment softened her voice. "You do?"

"I have meetings tomorrow morning that I can't miss. Italy is seven hours ahead. The flight is seven hours. I'll get there fourteen hours after I leave here."

She plugged the pod into the one-cup coffeemaker, regret flooding her. She should have pushed the night before. He was leaving. She had to stay here. God only knew if they'd see each other again. They'd missed their chance.

Still, she said, "I understand."

But when she reached into the refrigerator for cream, her ring glittered up at her. She had decided she could get the ring cut off herself, but she didn't have to. Doing it together was a valid reason for them to see each other again. All was not lost.

Her mood brightened. "Besides, my mom is fine. Or will be fine shortly. You can report back to your grandmother that everything is good."

He snorted. "Yeah. That will cement my story." He took a quick breath. "Which reminds me. There's one more thing."

She poured her cream in her coffee and faced him. "What?"

"Yesterday afternoon, while you were at the hospital, I found a jeweler here in Manhattan. Rafe recommended him. If you and I can be there at ten o'clock this morning, he can remove the ring."

"Oh." Her brightened mood tumbled into genuine despair. Without the ring there was no reason to see each other.

"It just seems prudent to get this taken care of while we can."

"Yes. You're right. I'm sure my mom's doctor will be there well before ten. Plenty of time for me to talk to him and then meet you at the jewelers." She took a breath. Confusion and a need to get away from him so he wouldn't see her disappointment made her babble. "Actually, he's there at seven or seven-thirty. So, I should get going. I'll see him and have plenty of time to get to the jeweler. Text me the address."

"I'll send my limo for you."

She headed for the door. "Sure. Great. I'll see you there."

CHAPTER NINE

Antonio stood in the office of Rafe's friend, Bruno, trying not to pace. The night before he'd sent Riley to bed—without him—after she'd made it clear she wanted to give in to their attraction.

He'd called himself crazy a million times. He'd gone over every event of the day, wondering what had held him back when everything he'd wanted had been at his fingertips.

And he got no clear reason for his hesitation.

He'd known she was tired, but making love had a way of invigorating people. Yet he'd walked away. Even after she'd very clearly said she understood anything between them would be temporary.

Something was definitely wrong with him.

Which was why he was handling the issue with the ring and returning to Italy. He had trouble enough maintaining a fake engagement for GiGi. He didn't need the added distraction of wanting to sleep with his fake fiancée, then walking away from the opportunity, making himself question his sanity. The truth was he was never supposed to see Riley again after his proposal. Instead, they'd been together nearly every day since their fake engagement. That was why everything felt so off.

He would go home and get back to normal. Without her around, the fake engagement would become nothing but telling GiGi that his visits to Manhattan were to see Riley. And his world would return to business as usual.

Bruno entered with a china cup on a saucer. Antonio hadn't really wanted coffee, but he was too antsy to make small talk with someone he didn't know.

"Your fiancée is here."

He took the coffee, setting it on the desk without even a sip. "She's arrived?"

"She's walking through the shop right now."

The door to the jeweler's office opened and Riley stepped inside.

She smiled.

His heart pitter-pattered. Tall and slender, she looked regal and elegant even in jeans. Her green eyes always sparkled. Her lips were full, perfect.

Regret tried to rise. He reminded himself that he needed to get back to behaving like himself. And he never seemed to do that when he was with her.

"Thank you for coming. How is your mom?"

"She definitely will be going home today." Riley laughed. "Her assistant has staff lined up to be with her 24/7. And she is in a mood." She laughed again. "She's awake and bossing everybody around."

"Then it's time for her to go home."

"Yes. Her assistant got her condo ready for her. I suggested my condo, but my mom refused." She laughed. "And not politely."

Antonio pictured her mother's reaction and laughed too.

Bruno said, "Shall we do this?"

Both Riley and Antonio said, "Yes."

Bruno had Riley sit at a small table by his cluttered desk. He slid a piece of plastic under the ring and caught Riley's gaze. "The plastic ensures that your finger won't be hurt."

She nodded. "I trust you."

"I've done hundreds of these."

He worked his magic and cut through the band, then pulled the two sides apart just enough she could slide the ring off.

She breathed a sigh of relief. "Thank you."

Antonio said, "Yes. Thank you." The same relief she'd obviously felt swelled in his chest. Their two-week engagement was over for her. He'd still be pretending. But now he had only his grandmother to manage. Not a grandmother, a fake fiancée and confusing emotions.

"The band can be repaired," Bruno said, handing the ring to Antonio.

He slid it into his jacket pocket. "Actually, I'm

thinking of having the diamond set into a pendant for my grandmother."

Not really understanding, Bruno nodded.

Riley rose from the chair, brushing off the front of her shirt as if she thought it had been covered in dust from sawing the band.

But Antonio didn't see any dust. All he saw was the way her shirt cruised over the swell of her breasts.

He shook his head to clear it. "Can I drop you at the hospital?"

"No. My mom's room is full of people. She's holding court as they wait for her discharge orders." She took a breath. "I could use a break."

Antonio put his hand on the small of her back to direct her to the door. "Okay. I'll take you to your condo then."

"Thank you. I would appreciate that."

With their relationship ending, she was behaving the way she had the day she'd planned his fake proposal. Professionally friendly. He remembered how much trouble he'd had keeping his eyes off her that morning in her office—and the night before. Something about her classic beauty had drawn him in a way no woman ever had.

The hand he had pressed against the small of her back began to tingle.

She led him through the posh jewelry store and onto the street, where his limo waited. The driver opened the door. She slid inside. He followed her.

As the car pulled into the street, she faced him with a smile. "This feels weird. Different."

"Actually, it feels like the morning we planned our proposal."

"Really?"

"Yes. I feel like myself again."

"Because you're not engaged."

"*We're* not engaged."

She chuckled, but their gazes met.

Something like hot honey poured through him, heating his skin, setting his blood on fire. They weren't engaged. There was nothing between them except an unrelenting attraction.

His smile faded.

Her smile faded.

Before he really knew what was happening, he was kissing her. Her hands were on his back. His hands tried to be everywhere at once. They drifted from her waist to her rounded hips and then back up again. He couldn't believe he was actually, *finally*, touching her and that she was touching him back.

Here they were, in a limo…doing what they'd both been aching to do. And it did not feel wrong as it had the night before. It felt right. Perfect.

She pulled back and he realized they'd arrived at her condo. Her sparkly green eyes glittered. "What time's your flight?"

"In three hours."

"It'll take an hour to get to the airport."

He slid his fingers under her hair, kissing her deeply, his tongue mimicking what every other cell in his body wanted to do before he pulled away and said, "We have time."

They exited the limo and said hello to that day's doorman as they tried to casually stroll to the elevator. When the door closed behind them, he braced her against the wall of the little car, sliding his fingers through the hair at her nape, holding her head exactly where he wanted it so he could kiss her the way he'd yearned to for two incredibly long weeks.

The door opened and they kissed their way down the hall to her condo. She opened the door. They stepped inside and he caught her to him again. Knowing the way to her room, he turned them in that direction and kissed her until they entered her bedroom. Then he reached for the buttons of her blouse, and she slid his suit coat off his shoulders. It tumbled to the floor. He didn't care. Her blouse joined it, then she undid the snap of her jeans and stepped out of them and her panties. He followed suit with his trousers, unbuttoned the top few buttons of his shirt and pulled it over his head.

Naked, they faced each other, then as if they were a magnet and steel, they came together for a passionate kiss. Blistering heat consumed him, especially when her hands drifted over his skin.

He kissed his way down her neck to her breasts and she groaned with pleasure.

Everything dissolved into a mist of desire. He wasn't entirely sure how they ended up on the bed or how he knew the exact minute to enter her. But the pleasure of it, the heat, roared through him. He understood why. He'd waited two long weeks for her.

Making love with Antonio was like stepping into a hurricane. At first, Riley thought she wouldn't be able to keep up, but something inside her snapped. Her days of being nice Riley, overworked Riley, driven Riley, were over. Except for making love to him. Then the desire that drove her to taste and touch him to her heart's delight was exactly what she wanted. When the pleasure crested and exploded, she closed her eyes and enjoyed.

After a few seconds of absorbing every feeling, she sighed with contentment. "Wow."

He rolled over, dropping his head to her pillow, pulling her with him so they could nestle together. "Yeah. Wow. That was amazing."

"It was." She half sat up. "But I was referring to how you must really not like being engaged."

He frowned. "Excuse me?"

"You had the restraint of a saint until we weren't engaged. But I took off that ring and boom. Everything exploded."

He thought about that for a second. "Really?"

"That's exactly what happened. You turned me down last night, remember? Then that ring came off my finger and we weren't in the cab ten seconds before we were kissing. Like someone had flipped a switch."

He laughed. "I did have a really, really, really God-awful marriage."

She laid down again, snuggling against him, and placed her hand on his chest. "So you've said."

"Because it's true. It was bad. Even before my wife cheated on me, our relationship had crumbled. I didn't realize it until I looked back on things, but she'd been out of the marriage long before I even knew it was over."

"Really?"

"I should have seen it when she became difficult. She loved living in the family villa when we first married. But six months in, she made me buy a house for us." He snorted. "Which, six months later, she took in the divorce."

"Oh."

"Don't say 'oh,' snarky like that. It was about more than money. At least to me. Before we were married, we talked. We made plans. She even wanted children. I genuinely believe that she loved me for the year we dated and the year we were engaged. But her love grew cold quickly once we got married."

"Unless she was just infatuated with you. Or eager to be married?"

Antonio laughed. "Neither. She loved me. But after almost three years, a year of dating, a year engaged, and a few months of being married, her love died." He shrugged. "Maybe from boredom. Or maybe familiarity?" He shrugged again. "Whatever the reason her love grew cold, it almost doesn't matter because it did."

"How about yours?"

"Have someone treat you badly long enough and your love would die too."

"I get that."

"Really?"

"I might not have been treated abysmally, but the last guy I lived with behaved more like a roommate. After a while our feelings dimmed, then suddenly my life was empty even with him in it."

"So *you've said.*"

She laughed. "Yeah. But the same as your wife, Chad had left the relationship long before I asked him to move out. I'm absolutely certain, he missed my condo more than me."

He glanced around appreciatively. "It is a nice condo."

She laughed, then slapped him playfully. "I'm more than a condo."

He rolled her to her back. "You definitely are. And if I had you in my life 24/7, I wouldn't spend more time with your big screen TV than you."

He kissed her and her chest filled with happiness. But kisses soon became caresses. Caresses fueled the fire of their need. And the second time they made love was more passionate than the first.

She could not imagine a woman growing tired of this…of *him*.

But she wouldn't let her thoughts go any further than that.

This was about them living in the moment. If she let herself start believing it could become something more, she'd end up with a broken heart. He'd been very clear that he didn't want to marry again. She wouldn't let herself fall into the trap of thinking she could change his mind.

Antonio knew it was time to head to the airport. As it was, he would barely make his flight. But he didn't want to leave. Of course, there was another option open to them.

He ran his big toe up her leg. "Come to Italy with me."

She laughed. "Right."

He sat up. Caught her gaze so she would know how serious he was. "Please. We can't have one time together and hope we somehow run into each other again when we live on two different continents. Come to Italy with me."

Her eyes shifted, as she absorbed that. "What about your grandmother?"

"What about her?"

"I don't have a ring. She can't see me."

"If we run into her, we'll tell her it had to be resized."

She bit her lower lip. "It's not a lie."

"No. It's the truth." He ran his finger along her arm. "Plus, you still have vendors to investigate."

"I do. But I also have a mom who is getting out of the hospital today."

"You said she was fine."

"I'd still like to watch her the first day or two she's home."

"So come at the end of the week."

She inclined her head. "I suppose I could."

He took a breath, waiting for her to think this through. They might not be together forever, but they had something special. No matter how short-lived, he wanted to enjoy it.

When she didn't say anything else, he decided to pull out the Salvaggio charm. "We'll have the whole weekend." He nuzzled her neck. "Please."

She laughed "You're very hard to say no to."

"It's part of my charm."

"No. It's the result of your charm…and good looks…and that damned accent of yours."

He rolled out of bed, glad she'd agreed. But because this was supposed to be casual, he wouldn't push for or promise any more than that.

"All right, you figure things out while I'm in the air and I'll call you when my flight lands. We can make plans."

"Those plans are going to have to include me

actually visiting the list of vendors Geoffrey made for me the other day."

It hit him in the oddest way that she called his assistant by his first name. It added a layer to what was happening between them that was fun and intimate. Though he would be careful with that. It was why he hadn't argued with her when she made the connection between getting rid of the ring and finally falling into bed together. It had given him a chance to further explain the story of his marriage. To make sure she understood why he would never again make the mistake of believing that love lasted.

After he'd redressed, she walked over and kissed him. "I'll miss you."

"I'll miss you too." He breathed in the scent of her, took in every detail of her face, memorized the sound of her voice…then kissed her good-bye.

She hadn't debated his view on love the way she had the night he'd slept on the chair in her little hotel room. She didn't make any proclamations or seek promises.

Finally, they were on the same page.

"I'm very glad things are working out between us."

She smiled. "I am too."

"And the fact that this is only us, in the moment, really doesn't bother you?"

She toyed with the button on his shirt. "I've

been so serious for so long I think something fun and frivolous is what I need."

He kissed her. "It's definitely what I need." He kissed her again. "I'll see you on Friday."

And *that*, he decided, was the reason he felt comfortable with her now. Not the loss of one engagement ring. It was the release of expectations and pretense.

Now, they had none. Only each other.

CHAPTER TEN

ANTONIO DIDN'T CALL the second his plane landed. He'd slept through the flight and awoke groggy. He intended to call her when he got to the villa, but his grandmother was up and waiting in the family room for him.

"How is Riley's mother?"

Knowing GiGi sometimes had trouble sleeping since his grandfather's passing, he kissed her cheek. "She's good. Today, she woke grouchy and bossy so her doctor told her she could go home."

GiGi clutched her chest. "Really? A grouchy, bossy woman is well enough to go home?"

"She owns a home nursing agency. Half her staff will be at her beck and call."

"She will be cared for?"

"Probably better than the rest of us are after a hospital stay."

She breathed a sigh of relief.

Antonio walked to the bar and fixed himself an old-fashioned. "I'm glad I went to Manhattan to check on things though."

"I knew you would be."

"In spite of her mom being in the hospital, Riley and I had a good visit." He couldn't believe how easily conversation poured out of him. He knew his GiGi wanted details, wanted to feel part of things, and it was wonderful that he really did have facts for her. No lies. Nothing to worry about remembering. Except—

"The only problem is her ring is at the jeweler."

GiGi gasped. "Why?"

"Basically, it was too small."

"So, Rafe has it?"

"No. It's with a friend of Rafe's in Manhattan."

"Hmm."

He fell to the sofa and sipped his drink. "It's all good."

"I wouldn't think a resizing would take more than a few minutes. A day at most."

"Well, this one will."

"You should have let Rafe handle it."

"It's fine. Riley's fine. You'll see for yourself when she flies over at the end of the week."

GiGi brightened. "She's coming here again?"

Antonio fought a wince. Drawing on the truth was one thing, but he never should have told her that Riley was returning to Italy. This visit was for them—to stay in bed for a few days. Enjoy what they have. Now she'd have to at least come for dinner.

He downed his drink and decided to end the

conversation before he fell into another easy trap. "We are a couple. We do miss each other."

She beamed. *"Si."*

He took his glass to the bar, kissed his grand-mother's cheek again and went to his room. He shucked his jacket and loosened his tie, then sat on the sofa in the sitting area of his suite and called Riley.

She didn't answer until after the third ring. He laughed. "Playing hard to get?"

"That ship has sailed. Besides, I think this thing between us will only work if we're completely honest."

"Okay. In the interest of honesty, I told my grandmother you were visiting at the end of the week, and she assumed that meant you'd be coming here for dinner."

She thought for a second, "I could come for dinner. I didn't take enough pictures of the potential proposal sites when I was there the other night. I didn't go into the winetasting room at all. Jake will need more than just my gushing descriptions when he updates the website. A visit over the weekend could kill two birds with one stone."

He laughed and relaxed on the sofa.

She relaxed on her sofa. For once a relationship didn't make her a bundle of nerves because it wasn't really a relationship. It was a short-term thing. She didn't have to worry about pleasing him beyond what came naturally. She didn't wonder if he wanted her condo. She wasn't on red alert trying to be a sparkling conversationalist.

She simply enjoyed him—enjoyed what they had in the moment.

They talked for another hour and that amazed her too. They were from two different cultures, two different worlds, but they had a million things to talk about. Making her believe the world really was getting smaller because of the internet.

She went to bed and woke early so she could visit her mom. To her surprise, Juliette was sitting at her dining table, with one of her staff serving her breakfast.

She pointed at her mother's plate. "Eggs and toast?"

"No one's worried about my cholesterol, Riley. It's my arm everyone wants to heal. And I'm taking advantage. I might even put jelly on my toast."

Riley laughed and took a seat at the table.

"Let me have Janine bring some eggs for you."

She almost said no but remembered what Antonio had said about her eating habits. That reminded her of the bowl of marinara sauce in her freezer and the groceries in her cupboards. Her heart filled with indescribable joy. Having someone who thought of her needs was weird, but in a wonderful way. Their relationship might not be permanent, but it still had its good points.

"I could eat an egg or two."

Janine came in and her mom asked her to bring two eggs and toast for Riley. When Janine was gone, her mom said, "So what's the big smile for?"

"Nothing. Just glad to see you're okay."

"I'm fine." She picked up her toast. "Are you sure it's not your Italian god who's making you smile."

She laughed. "He's in Italy."

"Too bad. I would have liked to get to know him."

"Really?"

"At first, I thought it was sweet that he faked an engagement to help his grandmother, then he seemed to be around you a lot more than a fake fiancé should." She pondered for a second. "Almost like he thought the engagement was real."

"His grandmother insisted he come here when she heard you were hurt." Janine served Riley's breakfast. "If he hadn't come, she would have gotten suspicious."

"Um-hmm."

Riley frowned. "What does that mean?"

"I don't know. There's something about this whole situation that makes me uncomfortable. A handsome guy who needs a fake fiancée? And why you? Why not bring one of his friends?"

"Because I was planning the proposal, he thought I would provide the fiancée and I thought he would bring a friend to pretend to be his fiancée. When we realized our faux pas, we also saw I was at the park and dressed like a woman about to be proposed to. That was your fault by the way."

"My fault?"

"You wanted me dressed up for your doctor dinner."

"Ah." Her mother frowned, then waved her fork. "You know what? Never mind. I'm on painkillers. All this suspicion is probably from being woozy."

"Probably."

Riley ate her breakfast, then left for work, where she got the totally opposite reception from Marietta.

Grinning like a fool, she caught Riley's arm and walked her down the hall to her office. "So? What happened?"

She frowned. "With my mom?"

"With the Italian dreamboat. What a great guy! So sweet and considerate."

"He is a good guy. But you were in on the ruse. We aren't really engaged, remember?" She displayed her bare hand. "In fact, we had the ring cut off yesterday."

Marietta frowned. "Really?"

"Yes! The thing was expensive, and it was weird walking around wearing it when it meant nothing."

"I don't know. I'm not sure it meant nothing. There was something about the way he looked at you that—" She shrugged. "Maybe it made me think there really was a spark between you."

There was a spark that had turned into a ridiculously hot flame. But Riley wasn't about to tell Marietta that. And there was indeed something odd about her relationship with Antonio, but it wasn't that he harbored real feelings for her. It was that Riley was doing something she never did. She had entered a relationship that didn't have a chance in hell of becoming permanent.

And she liked it.

She liked the freedom of it. No one, not even super romantic Marietta, was going to put doubts in her head, or turn her logical thought process into wishful thinking by suggesting that Antonio might want something more than a couple weeks or months of great sex.

He wouldn't.

She smiled at Marietta but as soon as her assistant walked up the hall to her office, her smile drooped, and she wasn't sure why. She and Antonio had a mutual agreement to keep things simple and temporary. And she *needed* a fling. Some fun—

Reminders of her real goals filled her head. Kids. Noisy breakfasts. Happy holidays—

She dismissed them. That was for another time. These next few weeks were for fun.

Friday evening, Italian time, she arrived in Italy to find Antonio waiting for her at the airport. He held a bunch of flowers, which he almost dropped when he grabbed her to kiss her hello.

He took her overnight bag from her and frowned. "I guess you're not staying long?"

She linked her arm with his. "Well, it's Friday night here, so technically, I can't do the work I wanted to."

"You won't be working this trip?"

"I'll work Monday and Tuesday…go home Wednesday morning, meaning I should be in Manhattan on Wednesday morning. I brought plenty of clothes, just packed everything into the bag snugly."

He grinned. "You're so clever, making time work to your advantage."

"I know!"

"Who's minding the store?"

"Marietta. I reminded her that your assistant had created a list of potential vendors for me." She shrugged. "I made it sound all business."

He laughed. "You're having too much fun with this."

She shook her head. "I don't think so. I missed out on a lot of fun. I think I'm just making up for lost time."

They reached his limo. The driver took her bag, and they slid inside.

"So, what's on our agenda?"

He settled back on the comfortable seat. "Tonight? Nothing. Tomorrow, GiGi is expecting you for dinner."

"So, we have tonight and all day tomorrow."

"Yes! And because we have all night and tomorrow, we're going to get dinner, then I'm going to show you at least some of the city before we retire."

They drove to her hotel where a bellman took her bag and the flowers Antonio had brought for her. He headed for her room and they went to the bar/restaurant with the glass wall.

"I hope we don't run into Marco again." He pointed at her hand. "You don't have a ring."

"It's at the jeweler," she said, smiling.

"Yeah. We might have to be careful with that. My grandmother mentioned that rings are typically resized in a day or two. It shouldn't take weeks."

"Okay. Maybe we just don't mention it."

He nodded. They ordered dinner, drank wine, ate a delicious meal, then took a stroll. The night air was perfect. June had become July and the temperatures had risen, but as darkness descended on Florence everything cooled. The scent of water filled the air.

"Is there a lake around here?"

"A river." He turned her to the right. "This way."

He led her down a few streets and a stone bridge came into view. "Ponte Vecchio."

"Oh… Ponte Vecchio," she said, mimicking his accent. "It sounds romantic."

"It means old bridge."

She laughed. "Apparently, people were more realistic when they named things back then."

"It's one of only a few bridges to survive World War II."

Arm in arm, they ambled over. "So, it's old and stubborn."

"Like my grandmother."

"She still hasn't scheduled her treatments, has she?"

"No. She's growing happier by the day though. I will keep up the ruse long enough for her to settle in, accept her happiness and get her treatments."

"As long as we're still, you know—doing this—I don't mind popping in to see her when I visit."

"Thank you."

"We'll have to figure out something about the ring."

"I still have it. Maybe I really will get it resized and you can slip it on when you visit."

"Sounds like a plan."

They stopped at a stone wall and leaned against it, looking at the reflection of the bridge on the water. Tourists milled around them. The sound of happy conversations floated on the air.

"This place is busy, yet it's peaceful."

"All of Italy is like that. There's a hum of something that rides the air. But it's something sweet and good." He chuckled. "Look at you, turning me into a poet."

"I think you could be anything you wanted."

"You do, do you?"

"You're smart. You're charming. And you seem

to be in tune with everything around you." She paused and smiled. "You notice things like my bare cupboards. And you solve problems by doing things like filling those cupboards."

His expression grew serious. "*Are* you eating?"

"I've always eaten. Now, I'm actually thinking before I choose. I'm still grabbing a donut for breakfast, but I'm not skipping lunch and I'm eating something healthy for dinner like a salad."

"I have changed you?"

Her mouth opened, but she stopped herself from admitting he'd done more than change her. He'd helped her shift from being a workaholic to being someone who knew how to enjoy her life while she ran her successful business. In doing that, she'd realized she could trust her staff more. In trusting her staff more, she could see her business had more potential to grow in the future.

It was like dominoes but different.

Still, there was no need for him to realize the huge impact he'd had on her life. Especially since she was barely a blip on the radar of his. That reminder tweaked her heart. But she stopped the shimmy of apprehension. They'd slept together once. He shouldn't have serious feelings for her, and she needed to keep her feelings and worries in check.

She turned to face him, and he pulled her into his arms. "Yes. You changed me...or my thinking. And I am happier for it."

"Being with you makes me happy too."

That was enough for her. She didn't have to be the love of his life. He didn't want a love of his life. He liked relationships but had no expectations. Technically, in this space of time they were perfect for each other.

Just two people having fun.

They strolled back to her hotel, both quiet. He seemed to be enjoying the atmosphere of the city closest to his family's vineyard. She was contemplative. Old Riley would be wondering about the end of their relationship right now. How she would cope. What her next step would be. New Riley realized that the woman who hadn't taken a vacation in a decade was on her second trip to Italy. With a man she wanted to be with. She refused to think about the future because there was no future. This relationship was about teaching her to relax.

They walked through the hotel lobby and to her room.

When she opened the door, he sniffed. "Really? You picked the same room you had last time?"

"Hey, being with you doesn't mean I no longer have a budget. I'm expensing this. I don't want the Internal Revenue Service to think I'm padding my trips."

He laughed and kissed her softly. But as always, their kisses heated and unwanted clothing disappeared. He caught the corner of the comforter and tossed it back.

"I'll bet two weeks ago you never pictured us sharing this bed."

She blinked. Had it only been two weeks? Good Lord, in fourteen short days, they'd gotten engaged, she'd met his family, her mom had been hurt. Her employees were now doing half her work. She'd become a world traveler. She'd started an affair.

He tumbled them to the bed bringing her out of her reverie. Her back arched as need sharpened.

But her thoughts sharpened too. For the first time in her life, she felt like herself. Not playing a role. Not working so hard she didn't have time to feel bad about her past. She was simply herself.

Or was she? This relationship was nothing like what she'd always wanted—

No. It was what she wanted, *right now*. She hadn't given up her dreams. Only delayed them.

Antonio kissed her again, running his fingers along her thigh. Everything inside her stilled, then came to vibrating life and she pushed those thoughts aside.

A ringing phone woke Antonio the next morning. He groped along the bedside table and grabbed it. Pressing the button, he answered, "Hello?"

"Where are you?"

"GiGi?"

Beside him, Riley stirred.

"Yes. Where are you? I thought you were bringing Riley home from the airport last night."

He ran his hand down his face to wake himself. "We're at her hotel."

Riley sat up. He mouthed, *It's my grandmother.*

GiGi's voice brightened. "Oh, so she did come to visit?"

"Yes."

"Let me talk to her."

"She might still be sleeping…"

Riley nodded and reached for the phone. Antonio said, "Nope. Wide awake. Here she is."

"Good morning, GiGi."

She put the phone on speaker, which was what Antonio would have been smart enough to do if he'd been more awake.

"Good morning, Riley! How is your mom?"

Antonio said, "I already told you that."

"I want to hear it from the source."

"My mom is fine. Great really. She has a nurse with her 24/7 and she's still tired enough that she's actually taking it easy." She laughed. "But next week, when she feels better, we might have to tie her down to get her to continue resting."

GiGi chortled. "She sounds like a pistol. I can't wait to meet her."

Riley's eyes met his. Her expression said she didn't want to lie. So, he said, "Pace yourself, GiGi, one Morgan at a time. You barely know Riley."

"And whose fault is that?"

"Not mine. I'm bringing her to dinner tonight."

"Good."

"But I'm not just here to visit," Riley said suddenly.

He knew why. She liked keeping the conversation on her business, so they didn't accidentally stumble into discussions where they'd have to lie.

"Part of the reason I'm in Italy is that I'm scouting vendors and venues for my business."

"Oh, the event planning!"

"Yes. Depending on the event, I need flowers and musicians and sometimes choirs."

"What kind of events do you plan?"

"All kinds," Riley said, and Antonio rolled his eyes. He knew she was avoiding mentioning proposal planning because it was just too close to their ruse.

"So, you're bringing your business here and when you are married, you will move to Italy?"

Riley blinked and Antonio stifled a laugh. His GiGi knew how to set conversational traps.

But Riley craftily said, "I can't live in Manhattan if my man lives here."

Antonio guffawed with laughter. Mostly because Riley was as crafty as his grandmother. Her answer had not been a lie.

Riley swatted him. He rolled out of bed and went to the bathroom, leaving Riley on her own. He wasn't helping much anyway.

Before he closed the bathroom door, Antonio heard GiGi's voice fill with excitement as she said, "You can tell me all about it tonight."

"Okay."

A minute later, Riley came into the bathroom. "I was just about to step into the shower."

"Oh, no. You're not stepping into the shower until you thank me."

He slid his arms around her. "For? You're the one who asked for the phone."

She sighed. "You're right."

"Besides you handled it brilliantly."

"She now thinks I'm moving to Italy."

He ran his hands down her bare back, luxuriating in the feel of her. "You do like it here. After you get this part of your business set up, you might actually want to move here. So, it's a possibility, not really a lie."

She kissed him, he was sure, to shut him up. Her moving to Italy was something they shouldn't even be considering. But unexpected happiness filled him at the thought, which wasn't at all what he wanted. What *they* wanted. This was temporary. And he would get them back to where they needed to be. Having an affair not thinking about the future.

Still kissing her, he reached into the shower and turned on the water, all thoughts of his grandmother forgotten.

CHAPTER ELEVEN

THAT AFTERNOON ANTONIO took the limo to the villa, giving Riley the afternoon to browse Florence while he went home to change clothes. She combined sightseeing with searching for the locations of the vendors on Geoffrey's list, though she didn't actually talk to any managers. She felt more like a tourist than a businesswoman today. Monday or Tuesday, she would make the contacts.

Today was for feeling happy. She refused to acknowledge the tightening of her chest when she remembered she'd never have any of the things she wanted as long as she was with Antonio. This was temporary. A respite. And she needed it.

When Antonio arrived to take her to the villa again, she was dressed in a pale blue sheath and white pumps. When he saw her, he whistled.

"You will wow my grandmother."

She glanced down at her dress. "No. This time I won't feel like a peasant."

He chuckled and they headed to the lobby, then out of the hotel to an Aston Martin convertible.

She stopped dead in her tracks. "Oh, my God."

"Pretty, isn't she?"

"She's… Wow."

"Now you see why I went home. I don't always like a limo. I love a drive in the country." He opened the door for her. "Climb in and get ready to enjoy the ride."

"How about if you climb in and enjoy the ride while I drive?"

He shrugged. "I don't see why not."

She just barely kept herself from gaping. Any guy who would trust a new person in his life with his fancy convertible either really liked her or he did not give a damn if she hurt his precious car.

Either way, she didn't care. She refused to think too deeply about anything when she was with him. That only led to reminders of what she would never have with him, and this wasn't the time for it. Right now, she wanted the luxury of driving his gorgeous car. She hopped in behind the steering wheel and pulled onto the street. He gave her a few quick directions that got them to the country road to the vineyard.

When they were out of the city, she hit the gas. The car took off like a rocket. The power was amazing.

She glanced over at him and shouted, "I love this."

"I love it too."

"It's titillating and relaxing at the same time."

"Exactly!"

The air swirling around them made conversation difficult, so Riley simply enjoyed driving, enjoyed watching the vineyards and villas that rolled along the gentle hills, the blue sky, the fresh air.

When they reached the Salvaggio mansion, they both climbed out. She walked around the hood of the car, caught Antonio by the back of the neck and yanked him to her for a hard kiss.

He laughed. "You're welcome."

"In bed tonight, you are going to be so glad you let me drive."

He laughed again and they entered his home. GiGi came down the curved stairway, again looking like mistress of the manor in a shirtwaist dress and pearls. She hooked her arm with Riley's, and they walked out to the patio.

"What did you do today?"

"Looked around the city. Antonio's assistant, Geoffrey, had created a list of venues for me. I didn't call them, but I did locate them." She took a deep breath as they stepped outside. "I just enjoyed being out and about."

GiGi smiled at her. "I hear Americans have difficulty relaxing."

"Antonio's helping me with that."

He walked to the bar, put wine on ice and rolled the cart to the chaises where they sat.

His grandmother shook her head. "He does

know how to get everything done and still have a good time."

Antonio's father, Enzo, arrived a half hour later. He got another bottle of wine. Though Antonio held back from drinking because he had to drive to the hotel, GiGi, Enzo and Riley drank it, talking about how Riley was expanding her business. Enzo gave her some insights and she wished she'd had a pen and paper because the man was brilliant, showing her exactly where Antonio got both his good looks and brains.

The sun began to droop. Riley glanced over and saw that their table had been set. She looked at her wine glass, wondering just how many of these things she'd had. Then she decided she didn't care. She was with people she liked, enjoying the conversation—

She *was* with people she liked.

People she liked a lot.

An overwhelming sense of connection swamped her. Not just a connection to Antonio or his family or the villa and vineyard. To all of it. The sense that she was coming home filled her so strongly her breath stalled.

She belonged here.

She belonged here.

Was Antonio right? After she set up this arm of her business, would she want to move here? And if she did, would she be Antonio's mistress forever? One day at a time, it would be so easy to continue an affair that worked and was so much fun. Especially, since talking about the future was off limits.

The thought fried her brain. It couldn't take a step forward or a step back as that scenario played out in her head. Sleeping together. Going out to dinner. Visiting his family. But never going any further than that.

She tried not to think about it, but the genie was out of the bottle. And he had brought a million questions. Most importantly, would bringing her business to Italy keep her connected to Antonio—

And would staying connected to Antonio change the direction of her life? Her plans?

Her real needs?

Kids. Noisy breakfasts. Weekends of soccer games. Snow white Christmases packed with gifts and laughter. Would she lose it all? Never have what she wanted?

She stopped the waterfall of thoughts.

That kind of thinking was something old Riley would do. That Riley was always looking to the future, trying to determine costs and consequences. New Riley lived in the moment. Too much wine had to be why she'd slipped back into that pattern.

She drank water through dinner, joking and talking with Antonio's family about the ups and downs of owning a company. Most of their wine-making business was handled by managers, but they still went to board meetings and heard about employee disputes and customer complaints.

With dinner done, Antonio excused himself.

Enjoying the evening, GiGi leaned back in her chair. "Such a lovely night."

"Everything in Tuscany is lovely."

She nodded approvingly. "You make my Antonio happy."

"He makes me happy."

"And when you have children, you will be even happier."

After a night of keeping the conversation away from personal things by talking business, Riley only smiled. But her waterfall of doubts returned. If she moved here—even if she simply made regular trips here for her business—would Antonio be in her life forever? And if he was in her life forever, would she give up her dreams for herself one day at a time, one visit at a time?

Carrying a duffel bag, Antonio stepped out onto the patio again. "Not every couple wants children, GiGi. Don't forget Riley is a businesswoman."

GiGi batted a hand. "You can hire nannies."

Looking exasperated with her, he shook his head. "Always practical."

"No. Just trying to keep you from being alone."

Ignoring that comment, Antonio kissed his grandmother's cheek. "We're going now."

"You will be back tomorrow?"

"I think I'm going to take Riley on an official

sightseeing tour." He offered her his hand. She took it and rose. He displayed the duffel. "That's why I'm taking extra clothes."

They left, ambling to the Aston Martin which still sat in the circular driveway. Antonio drove this time, happily shooting them up the country road back to Florence.

She appreciated the way Antonio had cooled his grandmother's expectation of children—promising the woman great-grandchildren when they might not even be a couple next year seemed more than one step over the line.

Then she remembered GiGi's response. She'd said she didn't want Antonio to be alone. Riley had realized that at the hospital, but hearing the emotion in GiGi's voice really cemented the idea in her mind. She didn't want great-grandkids as much as she wanted to make sure Antonio wouldn't end up alone.

But knowing GiGi as well as she was getting to know her, Riley also recognized that GiGi would adore any children Antonio had. She'd step into the role of great-grandmother like she was born for it.

Sadness for GiGi filled her. But she stopped it. That problem was Antonio's to deal with.

Just as her fear that she'd lose everything she wanted if she wasn't careful about this affair was her problem.

Suddenly, she couldn't stop herself from connecting what she was doing with Antonio to what her mom had done.

Was this what had happened? Her parents' affair had resulted in a pregnancy. They had a child. They committed—

But not legally.

And in the end her mom had been hurt. No. Her mom had lost everything.

She sucked in a breath, confused about why that comparison had popped into her head.

What she was doing with Antonio was different. There had been no promises. There would be no deciding they would get married "someday."

She would not lose everything, because she wouldn't allow herself to believe she and Antonio would ever commit.

Tooling around Tuscany the next day, she forgot all about that unfortunate comparison. What she had with Antonio was a straight up affair. She was having fun. Thinking such serious things was foolish—

Or old Riley ruining everything.

Luckily, Antonio made it easy for Riley to pause and enjoy herself as they puttered around town, ate lunch and did some touristy shopping. Monday and Tuesday, she worked with Geoffrey, interviewing vendors she could hire while working in Manhattan because no matter what impression she'd inadvertently given GiGi, she was not moving her company to Tuscany.

Not just because her engagement to Antonio was fake and therefore any planning that seemed to materialize when they were with GiGi was pure fiction; but because she was back to thinking realistically about this affair. Antonio had no place in her real-life decisions about her business. She was strong. She was smart. She had everything in perspective.

Especially the fact that she needed a frivolous affair. Something to get her sense of fun back.

All she had to do was withhold her heart. As long as she kept her wits about her, she could do that.

Wednesday evening, Antonio said good-bye to Riley at the airport and returned to the villa invigorated. It had been the best five days of his life. He couldn't ever remember working with such joy and efficiency. On Monday and Tuesday, he'd known he couldn't see Riley until the day's tasks were complete. So, he focused. And just when his jobs were complete, Riley and Geoffrey would return to the office, their visits to vendors done for the day.

She'd tell him about the vendors she'd found, the ideas she'd gotten, and they'd return to her hotel to make love. Then they'd wake up and do it all over again.

Every day had been fabulous, but he had to admit he was tired.

A voice in the back of his head reminded him that was irrelevant. Their affair was temporary, and he should enjoy it while he could. He and Riley would have fun for a few more weeks, a few more months…maybe even a year. Then it would be over.

His breath stuttered at the thought, but he reminded himself of his divorce, and his mother leaving and trying to get half the Salvaggio fortune. He remembered so much anger and pain. Strained silences in the villa.

The hurt of it rose as if both things had happened yesterday. He squeezed his eyes shut.

He would enjoy Riley while he could. Without dredging up those old memories. He did not need to be reminded that love didn't last.

In his own bed, he fell asleep and woke refreshed. Still, in the shower, alone, realizing he wouldn't see Riley that day or the next or the next, his mood plummeted. They hadn't made plans for her to return. He knew from her debriefings every day that most of her vendor investigations had been completed.

She didn't have any reason to come back.

He dressed, getting moodier by the second. They should have made some sort of plan, but they hadn't. Maybe she was already growing tired of what they had? Maybe it was time for him to bow out before he grew too fond of her, too accustomed to her—

The thought squeezed his chest.

GiGi and his father were already eating breakfast when he arrived in the dining room.

His dad laughed. "I'm hoping your mood improves before we have to meet with Marco this morning."

Not entirely sure what he'd done to clue his dad into his discontent, he mumbled, "I'm fine."

"No. You're not," GiGi said with a sniff. "You already miss Riley." She picked up her coffee cup. "Couples aren't supposed to be apart. You should get married."

Antonio choked on his toast. That brought him out of his funk really quickly.

"Married?" He almost reminded his grandmother that he and Riley had known each other three weeks—then he realized he'd led his family to believe they'd known each other longer.

Enzo frowned. "That's what engagements are for. Because eventually you intend to get married..." His voice trailed off as if that thought had reminded him of something. Or maybe because he was confused. Antonio's reaction to the word marriage had not been the reaction of a man engaged to be married.

Fear of getting caught rippled through Antonio. Before it could take root, he realized he was confusing their real-life affair and his pretend engagement. Talking to his dad and GiGi, he was engaged and should act that way.

He forced himself to perk up. "Of course, we're getting married. I was just thinking it would be more like next year. Or the year after."

GiGi sniffed again. "Two years?"

He dropped his napkin to his plate but took his coffee cup with him. He knew when a strategic retreat was necessary. It wasn't like him to get confused. It was time to leave and regroup. "This isn't a family decision. It's between me and Riley."

But just saying her name gave him a funny feeling in the pit of his stomach. As Gigi had guessed, he missed Riley. All those crazy memories about his marriage and his mom had pushed him in a bad direction and he'd reacted inappropriately.

He was *allowed* to miss her, but now that they were lovers, he was also permitted to do something about it.

"By the way, I'll be flying to Manhattan for the weekend. I hope we don't have plans."

Busy with his breakfast, his dad said, "No. No plans here."

His GiGi took a breath. "That's nice, but I was hoping she would come to Italy this weekend."

"She has a company to run and a mom who was just in an accident. We need to respect that. Plus, it's not very gentlemanly of me to expect her always to fly here. We'll be doing this fifty-fifty."

With that, he walked out of the dining room and returned to his room. He finished his coffee while talking to Geoffrey about flight arrangements for Friday. When the call was complete, he almost called Riley, but decided to surprise her.

Because that's what this relationship needed. Whimsy. Affairs were supposed to be fun, spontaneous. That's what he wanted. That's what she wanted. That's what they'd have. None of this worry that they would go too far. They wouldn't. He would see to it.

Even with video calls to her staff, the time Riley had spent in Italy had put her a week behind. She worked hard every day, then visited her mom every night. Not missing Antonio until she fell into bed exhausted.

Thursday morning, she wondered why he hadn't called and almost called him. She missed him. But this was an affair, not a relationship. Perhaps it wasn't proper for her to call? No. It definitely wasn't proper for her to call. Luckily, Jake came into her office with the prospective additions to the website, offering proposals in Tuscany. She shifted her mind off Antonio and onto work where it belonged.

Friday morning, she missed Antonio so much she knew she'd sound like a lovesick puppy if she called him, and he wouldn't like that. That wasn't their deal. She would not call him, not act like a real girlfriend. After all, she had plenty of work to do to get her mind off him. And she would do it.

But she still missed him.

Her company had a proposal in Central Park Friday afternoon and one at a restaurant Friday night. After the second one, she should have gone back to the office to continue catching up on work, but exhaustion and lethargy over missing Antonio forced her home.

This was the downside of a no-strings-attached love affair. He owed her nothing. Not even a phone call. She had no idea when she'd see him again.

Actually, she had no idea *if* she'd see him again.

Having an affair suddenly sounded like the worst idea under the sun. A confusing roller coaster that wasn't as much fun as it had seemed to be when they were together.

She missed him.

She wanted to tell him.

She wanted to see him.

But that wasn't their deal.

Tossing her purse onto the center island of her kitchen, she headed back to her bedroom to shower off her misery, but there was a knock on her door.

She frowned. Oscar usually called her if someone was on their way up. Shaking her head, she raced to the door, looked through the peep hole and saw Antonio.

She whipped open the door and he caught her to him, kissing her so hard and so fast, she lost her breath.

"I missed you."

A little stunned, she blinked. "I missed you too."

He walked in and she closed the door behind him. The second she turned, he pulled her to him again. This kiss was slow and languid, turning her bones to liquid.

When he pulled away, he sighed. "I would immediately make good on the promise of that kiss but I'm hot and sticky."

"Hmm. I was just going to go shower."

He laughed and caught her hand. "We are very attuned to each other."

Joy filled her. Not just because he was there, in her apartment, but because he had missed her. Maybe more than she had missed him because she hadn't flown across an ocean to see him but, here he was…across an ocean to see her.

The pleasure that filled her at seeing him tripled as they soaped each other in between heated kisses. They came together in a frenzy of need that reminded her of why this affair was such a good idea. Then they made love again before falling asleep.

Still, she hadn't forgotten that this was just an

affair. They could say they missed each other. They could be eager to make love. But after that an imaginary line formed. Not because he said so. Because this was what they had. Closeness but no commitment.

She enjoyed the closeness so much, though, that when they were together the lack of commitment seemed hazy, shadowy, so far off in the distance she refused to think about it.

She woke Saturday morning to the scent of bacon and grabbed a robe and stumbled up the hall to see him. She didn't want to miss a moment of him by sleeping away their time together.

When she walked into the kitchen, he kissed her. Realizing she was naked under her robe, he slid his hands inside, eventually easing the robe open so much that it puddled to the floor. He turned off the heat under the bacon and carried her back to the bedroom.

But while she enjoyed him being so hungry for her, he always seemed to be the aggressor, so she took over once they were in her room.

She leisurely helped him out of his shirt and pajama pants and when he would have pulled her to him in bed, she nudged his hands aside and straddled him.

"This is new."

She laughed, then kissed him. "You've pretty well taken control of things between us. It's my turn."

He laughed. She kissed him again, letting her hands roam. Then she slid her lips down his neck to his chest, enjoying the freedom he gave her to explore. But his hands slid up to her bottom, then up her waist to her breasts. She almost stopped him, but it felt so good she absorbed the pleasure even as she gave him pleasure.

But too soon he rolled her to her back and with a growl, nibbled bites down her neck. Her breath stalled, then jumped to double time when he entered her.

The heat and need and fun rolled through her like a happy symphony, until they reached the heights of excitement and anticipation and tumbled over the edge.

This was why she'd agreed to his insistence that this was temporary. She wanted fun. This was fun.

It was also why she could put her goal of a family on hold. This wouldn't last.

The following Friday, she flew to Italy. The week after that, he flew to Manhattan. Riley had promoted Marietta to office manager, and they'd hired a new assistant she and Marietta shared, as requests for proposals in Italy began to trickle in and their Manhattan business increased too.

Word of mouth was a powerful thing.

By the first week in October, they had a one weekend in Italy, one weekend in Manhattan schedule that they didn't even discuss anymore.

Every Friday night he either showed up at her apartment door or the door of her hotel in Florence.

The hotel staff got to know them. The restaurant knew she liked ketchup with her eggs. They didn't go to the villa every time she was in Tuscany. Having to pretend to be engaged was killing the romance of their fling. But every other visit she had dinner on Saturday night. This trip was her stay without dinner at the villa.

He woke up extremely happy and knew the instant she woke too. Instead of sliding together in a blissful storm of need, she rolled over and nestled against his side.

"What do we have planned for the day?"

"Since we don't have to be at the villa tonight, I thought you might like to take the train to Rome."

She sat up, her eyes as wide as saucers. "I'd love to."

"Let's shower first."

She laughed and got out of bed. Before they reached the bathroom door, his phone rang.

"I'm not even going to look at it."

She sighed, heading back to the bedside table and his phone. "How about if we see who it is." She picked up the phone and winced. "It's your grandmother."

He took it from her hands, sucked in a breath and smiled before he answered, so she wouldn't hear the exasperation in his voice. "Good morning."

"Good morning. May I speak with Riley?"

"If you're going to try to sweet-talk her into having dinner at the villa tonight, don't."

She laughed. "No, I will not mess up your dinner plans. I would like to have *lunch* with Riley."

"We're going to Rome."

"Go after lunch."

He shook his head. "No. I want to leave this morning, take the whole day. See as much as we can."

She sighed. "Okay. How about lunch tomorrow?"

"Lunch tomorrow?" Antonio said, glancing at Riley as he said it. His grandmother had capitulated rather easily, but Antonio wasn't about to question his luck. Still, he wouldn't answer for Riley and sent her a questioning look. She did that gesture Americans sometimes did, where they raised both hands as if to say, "What could it hurt?"

"All right. Riley's giving me a sign like she wouldn't mind having lunch with you tomorrow."

"Excellent!"

"We'll see you at noon."

"Not, we," GiGi corrected. "I want to have lunch with Riley alone."

Warning bells rang. "We're sort of a package deal these days."

GiGi laughed. "You can survive one lunch without her. Have her text me the name of the restaurant where she'd like to eat."

It gave him an itchy feeling to think of GiGi alone with Riley, but Riley was a pro. She could handle one lunch on her own. Actually, some days she was better at the engagement charade than he was. He could trust her.

He could trust her.

The thought rattled through him, then made him smile. He probably trusted her more than he'd ever trusted a woman he was dating. Certainly, more than he'd trusted his ex. They had to trust each other to keep their affair brief and on point. He should not be surprised,

"Okay."

"Grazie."

Antonio and Riley had their shower time down to a perfect balance of lovemaking and cleanliness. But today for some reason it all felt different. Probably because of realizing he trusted her. She was beautiful, soft, warm and happy. Which made him happy.

So damned happy.

Adding his happiness to the knowledge that he could trust her somehow doubled both emotions—turned them into something like joy.

In a moment of unguarded honesty, he acknowledged that he'd never felt this way before. Never.

But that could be because this fling was temporary with no chance for an ugly, unhappy ending. When it was over, there might be sadness—

Of course, there would be sadness. He would miss her, and she would miss him, but that would be much better than embarrassment and court battles.

No matter what he was feeling, it was okay. *They* were okay. In some ways, they were better than okay. All because he wasn't counting on their relationship becoming something that didn't exist. It was the most delicious affair he'd ever had, but it was still an affair.

Content with that explanation, he dressed and got ready to take her to Rome, where he had a hectic but fun day planned. His limo dropped them at Santa Maria Novella where they boarded the train and found their seats in first class.

She glanced around like a happy child, then sunk into the plush seat. "This is fabulous!"

"It isn't just comfortable. The train is fast. We'll be in Rome in about two hours."

"That's amazing." She turned to the wide window, obviously ready to watch the scenery fly by. "I love that your leaves turn colors like trees in the US. So pretty."

Antonio said, "Uh-huh," but he wasn't as relaxed as she was. Now that he'd sorted through his feelings about Riley, his brain switched over to wondering about his grandmother's sudden need for a *private* lunch. He'd been so preoccupied with Riley's end of things, he'd forgotten that his grandmother was crafty…a wild card. And she probably wanted something from Riley.

"You don't think my grandmother has an ulterior motive for having lunch with you, do you?"

"She likes my company and seeing me once a month isn't enough?"

Antonio's brain tried to absorb that possibility. As much as he wanted to believe it, he knew his GiGi too well.

Riley sighed. "Honestly, Antonio, is it so far-fetched to think she wants to get to know me? She does believe you and I are getting married—"

"In two years."

Her face scrunched. "In two years?"

"That's what I told her, remember?"

"I do now." She huffed out a sigh. "And that's her ulterior motive! She's going to try to talk me into marrying you sooner."

He laughed.

"This is serious! A potential landmine—" Her eyes narrowed. "Unless she's suddenly pushing because she's figured out our engagement isn't real?"

"How could she think that when we see each other every weekend? And we have to fly across an ocean to do it. We're obviously crazy about each other."

Riley pondered that for a second. "Maybe that's the problem."

"Seeing each other isn't good?"

"We're acting like people in a new relationship."

"It *is* new."

"No. You're not seeing it. We're not acting like people who are established. Settled. People who know they are going to see each other every day for the rest of their lives, so they have a certain security."

"We're not?"

"No. We have that glow of blissful ignorance."

He laughed again.

"You're still not seeing it. We act like people who think there's no tomorrow."

Antonio sighed with understanding.

They acted like people who thought there was no tomorrow because there might not be a tomorrow. Neither of them knew when this relationship would end, but it would end. So they enjoyed every minute like it was their last.

She was right. They didn't have plans. All they had was emotion. "We're acting like people who are madly in love." His voice shifted when he said the word love and their gazes met.

Was that what his changing feelings were all about? Was he tumbling over the edge from liking her to loving her?

He could not let that happen. He didn't want it for himself. He also didn't want her feelings to grow so much she got hurt.

She licked her lips and spoke slowly enough

that he knew she chose her words carefully. "I think it's more like infatuation."

He wasn't sure what she meant, but anything sounded better than love. "Infatuation?"

"You know. The shiny feeling at the beginning of a relationship. We don't see anything but good in each other and it makes us giddy. Engaged couples might be giddy but there's a substance to their relationship that tempers that."

"Oh." He saw it now. "And because we don't have that sense of being settled, GiGi thinks I'm postponing the wedding because I don't believe what we have is going to last?"

"Maybe."

His voice softened. "If she still has questions, she isn't buying this charade, is she?"

She shrugged. "I don't know."

He drew in a quick breath, as things fell into place in his head. "After three months of thinking I'm engaged, she still hasn't scheduled her treatments. Even with me and my father nudging her—reminding her that time is of the essence."

She caught his gaze. "Meaning, we're doing all this for nothing?"

"Not for nothing. She is happier. Much happier." He took Riley's hand. "And we do like each other."

She smiled. "We do."

"And tomorrow you have a chance to get her to talk. Maybe she'll tell you something? Maybe she'll explain why she's not getting her treatments. Maybe she'll alert you to the flaw in our plan?"

"Possibly."

"I think it's more than possible. If my grandmother wants to talk to you alone, it could be to get to know you better or trip you up. But think of it this way. That kind of conversation could lead her to talk about herself. And you could turn the tables. Be direct. Don't mince words. Ask the hard questions. And she'll either back off or explain herself. Either way we win."

"I guess."

"So, it's all good. Especially if you get her to talk. Then we can fix whatever she thinks is wrong." He squeezed her hand. "And today we can enjoy Rome."

Riley settled into her seat again. The idea that his grandmother wanted a heart-to-heart talk the next day was equal parts endearing and nerve wracking. So, she put it out of her head, determined to have a great day seeing Rome.

Seeing Rome.

A few months ago, she'd never left Manhattan, except for a few beach trips with her friends while on break from school. Today, she was on a train, watching the Italian countryside fly by. She'd come to Italy every other week for months. When Antonio came to Manhattan, they'd gone to Broadway shows, been to the Metropolitan Museum of Art, and most of the best restaurants in the city. Now, she understood what people meant when they said they were living their best life.

Four hours later, still awed by the scope of how her life had changed, she stood in Saint Peter's Square looking at the basilica on the sunny fall day. Antonio had rented a car so they could get in as many sights as possible. They'd stopped at the coliseum first, then driven to the Vatican.

Humbled by her surroundings, she glanced at Antonio who was trying to get a picture of her in the middle of the square alone. Every time he thought he had the shot, a tourist strolled by.

"Face it. You're not going to get a picture of me by myself. You're going to have to photoshop people out of the picture."

He gave up trying and took the picture as a mom and daughter walked by. "I forgot this is high season for tourists."

She strolled over and he slid his arm across her shoulders. "Because you're not a tourist."

He looked around. "Weather is perfect. Not hot. Not cold."

"So, people flock here," she said, interrupting him. "We're fine."

"That's what I like about you. No matter what's going on you find the good side."

"My mother taught me that."

"Oh, yeah?"

"She had to be positive." She shrugged. "Turns out it rubbed off on me."

"You are a ray of sunshine."

She laughed.

They visited the Vatican museums, the Sistine Chapel and the Vatican gardens, including Bramante's Belvedere Courtyard and the piece of the Berlin Wall. But by the time they were done, she was exhausted.

"That garden's huge."

He took a long drink of air. "And beautiful. Worth every step."

She laughed, then kissed him. She couldn't get it out of her head that she was in Italy, having fun, with a guy she really liked.

Thoughts of this relationship ending whispered through her brain, a gentle reminder to be careful. But she didn't want to be careful. For once in her life, she wanted to have fun. The kind of fun she could only have with a spontaneous, happy guy like Antonio. The affair would stop soon enough and that would be the time to be sad—or to actually begin looking for ways to accomplish her personal goals. Right now, she wanted every second of happiness she could have with him.

It was another twenty-minute walk back to their rental car. When they finally reached it, she stretched her arms above her head and stretched her legs out as far as she could in the small vehicle. "I'm going to be so happy to get into a hot shower."

He laughed and drove to the train station. Peace and contentment bubbled through her. She could not describe the feeling of actually walking through places she'd only ever seen in pictures or on television. But it was amazing. Her entire life had been amazing these past three months.

When they were settled in their train seats again, she squeezed his hand. "Thank you."

He laughed. "Don't you know, it's every man's pleasure to show his woman his world?"

She smiled at the way he called her his woman. A feeling of complete contentment rose until it filled her eyes with tears. She'd never met anyone like him, and she suddenly knew she never would again. She began the litany of reminders she usually ran through her brain when her thoughts got away from her like this, but the way her heart swelled would not be denied.

Some day she would lose him. He would walk away, and she would never see him again. It was their deal. She never dwelled on it. She didn't want to open the door to that trouble. But today, after his planning this wonderful trip, shepherding her through Rome and making her feel like the most important person in the world, she didn't see simple loneliness when their time together ended. She saw heartbreak.

Real heartbreak.

The truth tiptoed into her thoughts before she could stop it.

She *loved* him.

Oh, dear God. She loved him. Really loved him. She could see them spending the rest of their lives together. She could see their kids. Raising them on the vineyard. Taking them to Rome and Manhattan. Two different cultures, but culture all the same.

But he didn't want that.

Her heart squeezed and her breath stuttered.

She loved him and she had no idea what to do.

But she absolutely couldn't tell him.

Maybe it was a good thing she would spend tomorrow afternoon with his grandmother. She needed a pause to think all this through.

The real truth was it might be time for her to end it.

Her chest tightened so much she could barely breathe. How had she fallen in love with him when she knew it was wrong?

CHAPTER TWELVE

GIGI AND RILEY met at a restaurant Riley had suggested, somewhere close to her hotel, where she'd eaten lunch before. The day was cool, only in the high sixties, so she wore a yellow shaker knit sweater and jeans. But there was no breeze, so they could sit in the outdoor area, where GiGi already had a table.

GiGi rose to hug her and kiss her cheek. "Isn't this fun! Just the girls."

She laughed. Antonio hadn't talked any more about her lunch with his grandmother, but she was okay with that. She didn't want to have his suggestions and fears ringing in her brain during what might be a nice lunch with a woman she admired. She might not have to steer the conversation away from sensitive topics or ask difficult questions. GiGi might simply want a quiet meal with pleasant company.

That was what Riley wanted too.

After a good night's sleep, she had finally sorted out her feelings about her relationship with Antonio, realizing that when she'd come to her un-wanted conclusion that she loved him, she'd been tired. They'd walked what felt like miles. The Vat-ican Gardens themselves were fifty-seven acres. Of course, she'd had some unexpected thoughts. She hadn't been on her game. Her emotions had swelled, and she hadn't been able to combat them.

But now she was fine. She couldn't love a man who would never love her. Their affair would end. She would keep a lid on her feelings, so they could continue to enjoy what they had.

And she was happy to be having lunch with his grandmother.

"Is that why you didn't want Antonio to come with us? You want some girl talk?"

"That's part of it. You and I have never been alone long enough to have a real conversation."

"True." The waiter walked over, and she ordered a glass of wine, still looking at the lunch options.

GiGi handed her menu back to the waiter. "I'm just going to have a salad."

"Salad is good for me too," Riley said, also passing her menu back to the waiter. "What do you want to talk about on our girls' lunch?"

"Before we get into that. I did have an ulterior motive for keeping Antonio away."

She held back a wince. Maybe Antonio was right after all? GiGi had an ulterior motive in in-viting her to lunch.

"I wanted to tell you that I'm planning a surprise birthday party for him."

She blinked. "Oh."

GiGi waited as if she expected Riley to have a useful comment on that. But she couldn't think of anything to say. If his birthday was soon enough for his family to be thinking about a party, that was probably something he should have told her.

The waiter came with their wine. Riley took hers and gulped a big swig, buying time. She had no idea when Antonio's birthday was and clearly GiGi thought she did. Plus, a party meant meeting all his friends and relatives. That might even be GiGi's purpose of having a party. To bring Riley even further into the family.

She swallowed her wine and smiled at GiGi. "Really? A surprise party?"

"Well, not until his birthday next month. But with the schedule you two devised, I thought you could tell me which of the weekends closest to his birthday you'll be in Italy."

Two things struck her at once. With the party being a surprise, she couldn't tell Antonio why his grandmother had wanted to have a private lunch with her. Second, she wasn't sure how she would explain arriving a day early or on the wrong weekend—depending on when GiGi planned the party.

Still stalling for time, she smiled.

Drat.

This would not stump a real fiancée. A fiancée would know when his birthday was.

GiGi said, "I mean, the fourteenth is the obvious date. But if you're not coming until the twenty-first, that could work too."

"Or the seventh," Riley said quickly, trying to look like she knew when his birthday was. "It's better to have the party *before* his birthday…that way the surprise is real. He won't be expecting it."

GiGi laughed. "I like how you think."

Riley nodded, hoping she actually had gotten herself out of that without telling his grandmother she didn't know his birthday. The first thing when she returned home, she was asking him when his birthday was—

No. She couldn't do that either without him wondering why she suddenly wanted to know.

"Anyway, with that out of the way, you and I can have our girls' lunch."

She quickly scanned GiGi's face for signs she was going to spring something else on her. Seeing only a happy grandmother, Riley smiled and said, "Yes. We can."

Their salads arrived and GiGi opened her napkin, setting it on her lap. "So, tell me about your relationship with my Antonio. How did you meet?"

Deciding to trust her instinct that Antonio's grandmother was sincere and really did just want to talk, she took a breath. "Actually, we met at one of my events."

GiGi laughed. "Seriously?"

"I had planned an event for someone at a restaurant and he was there with…" She winced. "A date."

GiGi squeezed her eyes shut. "He was hopeless before he met you."

"No. I think he was just popular."

"Maybe."

"Anyway, he came to my office the next day," Riley said, sticking to the truth of their story. No lies. Omissions maybe, but no lies. "We made a date to see each other the day after that, and then we sort of fell together. I don't think it was love at first sight, but when we didn't have a date, we kept running into each other."

Which perfectly described her having to fly to Italy to tell him the ring wouldn't come off and then him showing up in her building when her mom was hurt.

"It was those unexpected meetings where we really got to know each other. No pretense like there usually is on a date."

GiGi laughed.

"Anyway, we might have gotten engaged a little sooner than we should have."

"You said when it's right you know it."

"Yes, I did." And thank God she had. "When he asked me to marry him, it just all felt right."

Which was also not a lie. It had felt right that

night in Dene Summerhouse. Weirdly right. But she wouldn't tell GiGi that.

"And you make good money with this business that you have?"

Riley smiled. She probably should have anticipated this question from the grandmother of a wealthy guy. She supposed a lot of women saw Antonio only in terms of his bank account. Riley could easily convince his grandmother she wasn't one of them. The man had her so bewitched she was worrying that she would fall in love with him for real. Their feelings for each other had nothing to do with money.

"Yes. My company is doing very well. With the addition of proposals in Tuscany, we're seeing an uptick in sales, but word of mouth for our New York business is also giving us new customers. Lots of people have events in Manhattan."

"I know. I've been to my share."

Surprise made her curious. "You come to New York?"

"I used to. My husband loved the city."

"So does Antonio! He said if there was a second place he would want to live, it would be Manhattan."

GiGi paused. "Oh."

"Not that we're thinking of living there," Riley said quickly. "I love Tuscany. Besides, we have plenty of time to think about that. Our wedding date is way in the future."

"I know."

From the sadness in GiGi's voice, Riley knew she disapproved. Maybe because of her grief over her husband, maybe because it seemed too far away to be real. That could be why she couldn't get excited enough to schedule her treatments.

She took a breath. She liked GiGi enough that she wanted answers as much as Antonio did.

"Is that why you haven't scheduled your treatments?"

GiGi could have been insulted by the question. Instead, she shrugged and said nothing. The woman who could talk for twenty minutes about a grape was suddenly tight-lipped.

Riley thought for a minute. There was really only one question that would bring GiGi right to the line of truth and force her to answer honestly. Difficult as it was, Riley decided to ask it.

"Don't you want to see our children?"

"Do *you* want to see your children?"

She assumed GiGi referred to the comment Antonio had made about them not having kids, and she knew she'd been right about pushing the conversation in this direction. Antonio had upset his grandmother with his offhand statement about not having kids.

That was why his grandmother had gone back to being depressed. She didn't not want to see Antonio alone for the rest of his life...and to an eighty-year-old grandmother, children were part of not being alone.

GiGi sighed. "Children bring happiness. Children speak of the continuity of a family. Your family is small, and you might not know this, but there is nothing like a child at Christmas. Or watching a toddler learn to walk. Or seeing the smile on their face when they see their mother."

Confusion overwhelmed Riley. She did know all that. She wanted a family so badly she'd tried to make three ill-fated relationships work. But Antonio had given his grandmother the wrong impression about her. Which might seem okay for the purposes of their fake engagement...but what if it wasn't?

Deciding to go with the truth, she quietly said, "I do want kids."

"You do?"

"Yes!"

"It's Antonio who is foot-dragging?"

She couldn't let his grandmother get that impression either. So she hedged. "We just got engaged. I think talking about having a family so soon made him jittery."

"Then maybe all this is just a matter of time for him to adjust?"

"Maybe."

She patted Riley's hand. "Definitely. Antonio might be stubborn, but he always comes around."

Riley laughed. "Antonio having a family really means a lot to you, doesn't it?"

"Of course! You and Antonio are so young you don't understand what it is to end your family's line, how alone he'll be. I have my son, Enzo. I have Antonio. But then our line stops. Enzo will have no more children, but he has Antonio. If Antonio doesn't create some heirs, he's going to be the one who is alone. Alone on our beautiful vineyard with no one to leave it to when he dies."

Riley opened her mouth to contradict GiGi, but nothing came out. If she fast-forwarded Antonio's life, if he continued to live the way he was now, he *would* someday be a very wealthy old man with a beautiful vineyard and no one to share it with—

Not her problem.

Not. Her. Problem.

The only thing Antonio asked her to do was figure out what was bothering his grandmother, and Riley believed she had. It was time to pull back. Not ruminate on GiGi's fears for Antonio. When she pictured him alone, those feelings she'd had the day before crept back and she didn't want them. She did not want to love him. She didn't want to feel so much for him that the end of their relationship would crush her.

She had to be smart.

"I'm afraid he gets this from his father, who also didn't remarry after a bad divorce."

Scrambling for a way out of this conversation, Riley said, "Oh, yeah?"

"Like his father, Antonio married a beautiful woman with no substance." She snorted. "Trophy wives, both of them. But I see the emotion in your relationship with Antonio."

Try as she might to stop it, Riley felt the emotion between her and Antonio too. She'd never had so many deep, important conversations with any of her exes. She'd also never had a boyfriend who cooked for her, cared about her mother—

She put the brakes on those thoughts. She could not keep reminding herself why she liked Antonio. Why that liking was beginning to tumble over into deeper feelings. She had to establish some boundaries.

GiGi laughed suddenly. "You and Antonio are so perfect for each other. He will come around about having kids and I don't have to worry."

Riley smiled, her emotions under control again. She liked Antonio so, so much but she was holding her heart in reserve. Saving that for the guy who wanted to be her partner, the father of her children, the guy who'd laugh at her gag gifts at Christmas and take her and the kids to the beach for vacations. Yesterday's unwanted feelings were an anomaly. She was smart enough not to fall for another guy who didn't want what she wanted. Everything was fine. Better than fine because she now knew what had been bothering GiGi.

She managed to shift the conversation enough that they laughed through the rest of their lunch. They talked about fashion, the movies they'd seen and Antonio's Aston Martin.

She hugged Antonio's grandmother good-bye and was fine on the walk back to the hotel, but as she stepped into the lobby, guilt crept up on her. She might be fine. And GiGi might be fine. But the real bottom line to their conversation finally emerged through the haze of her thinking. GiGi didn't want Antonio to find a wife so he'd be happy. She was trying to make their family whole again. She wanted him to have children so he wouldn't be alone.

Meaning, when they broke off their fake engagement, GiGi would be back where she'd started from. Sure, she would probably be through with her chemo by then and be well again. But she would fall back into that black pit of depression.

Riley took a breath, weighing options. Really, this was Antonio's problem, but she couldn't help recognizing he didn't have many options. His first priority had to be getting his grandmother well. After that he would have time to deal properly with her grief and depression.

Her room was empty when she stepped inside, but she barely had time to wash her hands before Antonio walked in.

"How was lunch?" He tossed his jacket to one of

the chairs by the little table with the phone. "Did she ask questions about us? Try to trip you up?"

"Your grandmother isn't an evil genius."

He laughed. "No. I think she's a normal grandmother. She just sometimes has a way of making conversations work for her."

She frowned. "I don't think she was doing that this time. She very sincerely told me that she worries you will be alone. She wants you to have children."

"Seriously?" His eyes widened. "*That's* what's bothering her?"

"Yes. One night after dinner, you casually said we wouldn't be having kids—because I'm a businesswoman."

He grimaced. "Yeah. I remember. I was just trying to stop her from steamrolling us."

"You might have stopped that but now she thinks you're always going to be alone."

He sat on the bed. "She's worried about me?"

"Yes. She sees you old and all alone on the vineyard."

"She's obsessing over nothing. I'll be fine."

Riley wanted to agree with him, but she saw what his grandmother saw. Young and handsome, he had no qualms believing his busy, happy lifestyle would last forever. But she knew it wouldn't. She'd lost her dad. She almost lost her mother. Life was tricky. One minute it could be fine and the next everything could fall apart.

"I'll just drop it into conversation one day that I think you and I will make great parents and that should fix it."

"It might."

"It might?" He frowned. "Are you thinking we should do something more?"

She shook her head. "Not we. *You*. How long's it been since you had a real talk with your grandmother?"

"About what?"

"I don't know. Your grandfather? How she feels about having lost him? Why she's so worried that you're going to be alone?"

He pulled in a breath. "We talked right after my grandfather died. We actually talked about you once. But it's been a while."

Guilt and sadness for GiGi filled her again. "Honestly, Antonio, I think she's lonely."

He ran his hand along the back of his neck. "Her best friend died last year."

"And she lost your grandfather this year?" She gaped at him. "She's definitely lonely. You need to spend more time with her. Quality time."

"You Americans and your quality time. Italians know how to be family. I will ace this."

She laughed and walked over to where he sat on the bed. He slid his hands up her bottom to her waist.

Ignoring the blissful sensations tumbling through her, she said, "You had better."

"Seriously. I'll talk to her. Maybe I'll even take her somewhere nice for dinner one night. Without my dad. I'll make it feel like a date."

She smiled, then kissed him. "You're a wonderful person." Was it any wonder her feelings were trying to shift from like to love? And was it any wonder it was getting harder and harder to stop them?

"If I were a wonderful person, I probably would have thought of this myself."

"Maybe."

He rose from the bed to kiss her properly and she gave herself over to it. But because it was Sunday, she pulled back.

"I have about an hour to get to the airport."

He sighed. "In all the worry about your lunch, I forgot you have to leave. Can't you stay another day?"

She shook her head. "No. There's a tsunami of Halloween proposals happening this week."

His face scrunched. "Halloween proposals?"

"Sorry. Everybody's obsessed with witches, zombies and skeletons these days."

"That's one of those things I'll never understand."

She laughed, kissed him, then started packing her bags.

On the plane, she settled in to fall asleep. Traveling to Europe every other week, she'd learned to book a seat in first class so she could make good use of the time. She arrived in Manhattan seven o'clock on Sunday night and putzed around her house, doing her laundry, beginning to tidy up for when Antonio would visit that weekend.

She'd talked herself out of falling in love—even stopped herself before she actually fell. Still, she liked him so much that she refused to waste any of the time they had together tidying up while he was visiting.

After all, any weekend could be the beginning of the end.

Their relationship had begun with a fake engagement to make his grandmother happy. Sure, they'd started a real affair, but it was still wrapped up in that fake engagement. If Antonio and his grandmother talked all this through, they wouldn't need the fake engagement anymore.

And the real-life affair might crumble with it.

She sucked in a breath as sadness rose at that thought, but she forced the feeling away. That was a worry for another day.

But the sadness wouldn't leave because deep down she knew they were at the beginning of the end.

CHAPTER THIRTEEN

ANTONIO TOOK HIS GRANDMOTHER to dinner on Tuesday night. He'd told her about the date on Monday morning, so she had time to prepare and anticipate. It was the happiest he'd seen her in months.

At dinner she talked more than she had since his grandfather's death. She didn't mention her grief. Her conversation revolved more around the past. What a precocious child he'd been. How she'd struggled to find her place in Tuscany's social circles. How Antonio's father had botched a marriage but become the best businessman she'd ever known. How Antonio clearly had his skills and abilities and would keep their companies thriving.

He didn't see the sadness Riley had seen. Tonight, she was bubbly. But he also didn't doubt Riley. If she'd said his grandmother had been struggling emotionally, then she had been.

As dessert was being served, he took her hand. "So, you are feeling better?"

She pulled back her hand and fussed with the linen napkin on her lap. "I'm feeling much better... thanks to Riley. The girl has nerve. She flat out asked me some questions like why I didn't want the chemo and she forced me to think."

He wasn't sure if that was good or bad. He sat back in his chair. "Oh. Have you made a decision?"

"Actually, I'm still thinking."

"How can you still be thinking!" Confusion overwhelmed him before he could stop it. "There's so much life to live!"

She shook her head. "You forget I've been through these treatments once already. I know how sick I'm going to be. I know the toll it takes. I'm nearly eighty. My brothers and sisters are gone. My best friend passed." This time she caught his hand. "Now, your grandfather is gone. He was not my reason for living. But I had a whole world of people when I went through chemo the last time. I had a good life. I had things I wanted to accomplish. Now, I wonder if my time is over. Other people took my seats on charity boards, and they are doing well. Your father is handling the company brilliantly. What he doesn't do, you do. I sit on a chaise longue and wait until it's time to dress for dinner."

She shrugged. "While I sit there, I think about the good life I had. The good things I've done and I'm proud. But I also see it's over."

He'd thought her reminiscence at dinner had been nothing more than a pleasant conversation. Now, he understood why she'd spoken of things long gone. She only saw her past. Not her future.

"It's wrong to think like that, when Dad and I need you."

"For?"

"Not *for* anything. *Because.* Because we love you."

"Oh, Antonio, I love you too." She shook her head. "So much. I remember you being born. I remember your coo. I remember your baby smiles." She chuckled. "It wasn't a hardship when your mother left. I was very happy to raise you."

"Then get the treatments for me."

She shook her head. "No. This choice is only mine. It's why I'm thinking it through so long." She laughed. "Though I have to admit, the thought of you and Riley having children does give me a boost of hope. Something that makes me want to see it."

"Then go get the treatments."

She took a breath. "I understand that to you this seems like an easy choice." She patted his hand. "When you are my age, if you are alone, if everyone who made your world a wonderful place is gone...only then could you understand."

"You're saying you're lonely."

"Give me a few more days to think about what

I want. Not what *you* want. Not what your father wants. What I want. I will decide soon."

Friday night when Antonio arrived at Riley's condo, instead of their usual kiss, he just hugged her.

When he finally pulled back, he said, "She's not going to get the treatments."

Riley's eyes widened. "She's not?"

"Well, she says she hasn't really decided yet."

She studied his eyes. "Then there's still hope."

"No." He flopped down on her sofa. "We had a talk. A wonderful dinner filled with lively conversation. Then she told me that her whole world is gone. Everyone who made up her life has passed. The essence of the conversation wasn't that she had nothing to live for but that she was done. Her time was over."

She sat beside him and took his hand. "Yes. But she also said she hasn't made up her mind."

He bounced from the sofa. "This is hopeless! For months, I've been trying to get her to see reason and I had absolutely no impact on her."

She shook her head. "I'm going to have to disagree about your trying to get her to see reason. You haven't been trying to get her to see reason. You faked an engagement."

His face sharpened. "Excuse me?"

"We aren't engaged. We aren't going to have kids. You really haven't given her anything. Not a wedding. Not great-grandkids to spoil. If a person looks at this the right way, you tried to trick her into doing what you wanted."

"I tried to give her hope!"

"Yes. And that's commendable, but, Antonio, there really wasn't any substance there." The truth of that swamped her. "We aren't going to get married. We aren't going to have kids."

"Oh, God." All the blood drained from his face as if he finally saw her point. "You're right." He looked at her. "I feel so connected to you that I sometimes forget that our love affair is one thing, our fake engagement is another."

She squeezed his hand. "Don't feel bad. The other day, in Rome, I had this flash of love for you that was so real I had to worry that I was tumbling over the edge."

His face changed. "You thought you loved me?"

She couldn't tell if he was confused or concerned. "Don't worry. It passed."

"It passed?"

"I talked myself out of it."

His gaze lingered on her face as he digested that. A few weeks before, the very idea that she might have genuine feelings for him would have concerned him. Today, he said only, "Oh, okay."

She swore she saw a flash of disappointment, as if her loving him had pleased him. She wanted that to be true. Maybe so much that she could be imagining it, so she didn't allow herself to dwell on it and changed the subject. "But to get back to your grandmother, I think we have to admit the fake engagement failed and look for a new strategy."

"It's hard for me to believe it out and out failed when she seemed so happy at dinner."

"She was happy because she had *you* with her." The truth of that washed through her. *She* was always happier around Antonio too. She missed him when they were apart.

She shook her head to get rid of that observation, afraid of where it was leading. "You're someone to talk to. Someone she knows loves her. Maybe that's more of what she needs?"

"She needs more going out to dinner?"

"No. More of you talking to her. For real. Instead of a fake fiancée and pretending you'll give her great-grandkids, maybe she needs more of you?"

Again, she saw herself, not GiGi. That was the truth of what was happening to her. She desperately wanted to take the next step. Say she loved him. Consider a future together. That's why it was harder and harder to shove down her feelings for him. They were at the place where they should be taking the next steps—

But it wasn't what he wanted.

She rose and took a breath. "In fact, I'm starting to see something that we missed." They'd missed lots of things but right now they were talking about his relationship with his grandmother.

This was what he needed to hear. So she stayed on topic though other things began to sort in her head. "She lost her best friend and her husband. What she needs is help building a new life. And I'm going to send you back to Italy right now to help her."

His face twisted with confusion. "Right now?"

"Right now. That was the real purpose for us getting together. You wanted to help your grandmother."

"And you're saying I need to help her rebuild her life?"

"Yes. Go. Help her for real."

He rose and caught her hand before she could turn away. "Come with me."

She smiled. "No. Think it through. She might like me, but you're her family. This is something you have to do."

"But she thinks of you as family."

"Because she thinks we're engaged. We're not. And I won't muddy the waters for her anymore." She took a sharp breath. Her thoughts cleared some more as logical conclusions began to form. "Even we had trouble keeping track of what was real and what was fake. I think it's time you get back to reality. Completely." Her chest froze, as the final pieces of the puzzle snapped together. She tried to avoid it, but she knew this was right. The thing he needed to hear. The thing *she* needed to realize. This was the end of their relationship.

She wanted to take the next steps. He didn't. If she didn't end it now, she wouldn't be able to. She would hold on. Start hoping for things that couldn't be—

The pain of it steamrolled over her. But she held her head high and said what needed to be said. "The best way to do it is to stop seeing each other."

His face scrunched. "Are you saying we're through?"

It hurt her to think it, but no matter what her heart felt, her head knew this was it. The end. She'd fought so hard not to fall for him, trying to hold on to what they had or enjoy what they had that she'd missed the obvious. If she didn't end it now, it would kill her to lose him later.

"Yes. This is over."

"But we like each other. We're good together."

"Yes. But we said when it was over, we would know it and we would be smart."

He blinked at her. The strangest feelings washed through him. "You are breaking up with me."

"Antonio, we were never really together."

"We weren't? We've seen each other several times a week since June. It's October. That's *together*."

"No. That was convenience and fun. Not commitment. We'd always known it would end. We made no plans because we each want different things out of life."

He studied her face. She was so sincere that it was difficult to believe she was the one ending things. Especially since she seemed so broken. Her words were blunt and to the point, but he saw the sorrow in her eyes. She'd said she'd worried she'd fallen in love for real and had talked herself out of it. But from the shadows in her eyes, he didn't believe she'd done such a good job.

She loved him.

Yet she was pushing him out of her life?

That didn't seem right.

The suspicion that hit him almost made him gasp. His eyes narrowed. "Are you angling to get me to ask you to marry me for real?"

"No!" Surprise replaced the sorrow in her eyes. "Even if you did, I wouldn't accept. You don't love me. You're just having fun. And, honestly, Antonio, there was nothing wrong with that. You're so happy when we were together that I loved being with you." She took a breath and the pain returned to her eyes. "But we've both always known that you don't want what I want. I want a partner, kids, a real family. You like your freedom. Standing here right now, knowing my feelings for you and that we'll never be on the same page, is killing me. So, I'm not just sending you home to do right by your grandmother. I'm sending you home because if we keep this up, we're going to hit a point where I'm not going to be able to come back from the hurt."

She blew her breath out. He could see the struggle going on inside her. "I'm going to take a walk. When I get back, you should be gone."

She headed for the door, but stopped suddenly and grabbed her purse from the center island. With money and credit cards she could slip into a bar and be gone for hours. She walked out into the hall and the door closed behind her, basically telling him there was no point in waiting for her to return.

They were done.

He stared at the door for a few seconds. Feelings, the likes of which he'd never before felt, bombarded him. He hated her pain. Hated that he was the one who had caused it. Wanted nothing more than to run after her and promise her whatever she wanted. But he couldn't. He couldn't walk into another relationship when he knew love always ended.

And she knew that. That's why she'd gone. They wanted two different things. Which was also why they'd so clearly defined their affair and knew it had a shelf life. Her feelings had crossed the line to love, but she understood that was a line he would not cross.

Now he also understood that his grandmother needed him more than he'd been around lately.

His affair with Riley might have been good

intentioned, but he'd spent time with her that he should have spent with his grandmother.

Riley had seen that.

She'd told him that.

She'd sent him home for all the right reasons.

He grabbed his duffel and left, ignoring the tightness of his chest and the sadness that rippled through him.

He knew how to be strong. He also knew it was time to do the right thing for real.

CHAPTER FOURTEEN

RILEY RETURNED TO her condo building hours later, still shell-shocked that she'd broken things off with Antonio. The affair had been the best time of her life, but she'd known all along it wouldn't be permanent. When she'd made her arguments for breaking things off, she'd seen in his eyes that he didn't love her. As much as she recognized that his grandmother needed him, knowing that he didn't share her feelings—would never share her feelings—was what pushed her to send him away. If she didn't end things now, she'd one day find herself so in love with him that losing him would paralyze her.

Or she'd move her office to Tuscany and always be a mistress.

She tossed her purse to the kitchen island, not quite sure how that could be worse than what she felt right now. Ending what they had hurt so much she could barely breathe. Add her feeling of foolishness to that and she almost couldn't function the next day at Saturday afternoon's proposal and thanked God Marietta took over. She improved somewhat for Saturday night's proposal, but not much.

She'd thought she'd known better than to fall in love with him, but she obviously hadn't been as immune and objective as she'd thought.

But how could she not fall in love with him?

He wasn't just good looking and suave. He was kind, thoughtful, fun to be around.

But he was adamant about not falling in love again.

She'd seen that in his eyes when she'd asked him to leave. They'd been so preoccupied with his grandmother that they'd downplayed his insistence that he wouldn't fall in love or commit to another woman. Because he'd been hurt. And he'd drawn a line in the sand, a line he'd never cross again. While she'd fallen in love naturally, it hadn't even entered his mind.

She entered her condo and walked past the kitchen, refusing to turn on the lights. It might be a while before she could look at the kitchen without remembering him happy, charming, cooking for her.

Heading back to her room for a shower, she called her mother to check in.

"Where were you tonight? Out with Antonio?"

She would have laughed at the snarky way her mother said his name, but her mother had been right. At first, she'd laughed about the fake engagement but eventually she'd noticed that there was something off about their feelings for each other. Busy with physical therapy and running a company from her dining room, Juliette hadn't had time to interfere. Riley had seen it as a gift from the heavens. But just as Antonio had to be honest with his grandmother, it was time for her to come clean with her mom.

"You can rest easy. Fake engagement is ended."

"Really?"

"Why so surprised? You seemed to see right through it all along."

"What I saw was you actually liking some-one, actually giving someone a chance. I honestly thought you'd come home some day and tell me you really were engaged."

She blinked. Had her mother not interfered be-cause she was rooting for them? She didn't know whether that was sweet or confusing. "Nope. The opposite. Our deal is done."

"You broke off a fake engagement and you're sad?"

"It was a fake engagement and a real love affair."

"You slept with him."

"What did you think I was doing going to Italy every other week?"

Her mother took a long breath. "I don't know… I've been so busy the past months went by in a blur." She took another breath. "Catch me up."

"We thought the fake engagement was over, started a love affair and got dragged back into pretending to be engaged when I was in Italy. After a while it sort of got confusing. We were pretending for his grandmother that we were getting married and alone we were having fun."

"I can see how that would get confusing."

"Yeah, well, when his grandmother broke down and started explaining why she didn't want chemo, I saw that even her grandson getting engaged hadn't perked her up."

"Really?"

"Her husband died this year, but her best friend died six months before that."

Her mom sighed with understanding. "She's alone."

"Really alone. And instead of faking an engagement, her grandson should have been helping her build a new life."

"I get it."

"That's why I sent him home. I ended the fake engagement and the love affair. It wasn't going anywhere anyway."

"But you were happy."

"Yes and no." The answer made her think of Antonio and her heart hurt. She'd never had what she had with him. She'd never felt what she'd felt with him. Her feelings had been strong and real… no matter how much she'd tried to fight them. Which was part of why it hurt so much that he didn't return those feelings. It seemed wrong to love someone and not have them love you.

"I always knew what we had wasn't permanent. His first marriage was a mess. He doesn't believe in love or commitment."

"That *is* a mess. Maybe you're lucky to get out of it?"

She blinked back tears and said, "Yeah. Maybe I'm lucky." But she didn't feel lucky. She felt sad. Sad for his grandmother. Sad for him. Sad for herself.

Because the other thing she wouldn't let herself think about until now was that she might have fallen so hard so far because she was lonely too. Vulnerable.

She should have kept all that in mind before having a torrid affair with a handsome stranger who did end up breaking her heart.

Needing time to sort through everything Riley had told him, Antonio had kept his return to Italy a secret by staying in Florence that night and Sunday. But on Monday, he couldn't avoid his grandmother another day. Plus, he agreed with Riley. He needed to help her. Not avoid her. A little honesty would get them on the right track.

Rather than eat outside, they chose to have dinner in the formal dining room.

He kissed her cheek, said, "Hello," to his father and took his seat. Jumping in feet first, he said, "Riley and I broke up."

Looking shocked, GiGi said, "What?"

"You didn't notice that I didn't spend any time in Manhattan because I stayed in the city the last two nights."

His father said, "Why?"

"This was hard for me."

"Because you loved her!" GiGi said. "Fix this right now. Go get her."

"No. I'm a grown man, GiGi. I know when something is over, and this is over. Besides, she broke up with me."

His grandmother gasped. "I don't believe it. That woman loved you! For the first time ever, I thought you'd finally found real love and you're letting her get away?"

"She told me to leave." Just thinking that hurt him. Still, he wouldn't let himself examine that feeling. Their relationship was a jumble of odd things. First, pretending to be engaged. Then becoming friends. Then taking off the ring and having something that felt real—

Then her telling him to go back to Italy. Easily.

No. Not easily. He saw the hurt in her eyes. That's what had made him stop arguing. She loved him and he did not love her. The gentleman in him wouldn't persuade her to continue a relationship that was no longer equal. He would protect her from himself.

No matter how confusing the constant pain in his heart.

* * *

Two weeks later, he'd managed to stop the pain. Or at least dull it with logic. His grandmother no longer hounded him to call Riley. They'd had more than a few good talks. He'd taken her to dinner at fancy restaurants. Once at lunch he'd invited one of her old acquaintances and they'd talked for hours.

That's when he'd seen his grandmother's spark really coming back. She'd also decided to have the chemo.

Not for a chance to see her great-grandchildren… but because she was beginning to see the good side of life again. He'd shown her that. Because Riley had told him to do it.

He squeezed his eyes shut. Soon, he hoped, everything in his life wouldn't remind him of her.

When GiGi asked him to dress for dinner the following Friday, he'd complied, if only because it meant she'd invited a guest. Which was another good sign.

But as he walked down the corridor to the curved stairway, the pain hit him again. Out of the blue, the feeling of his heart being ripped in half stopped him in his tracks. Riley should have arrived that evening. He should walk down these stairs and see her entering the foyer.

The thought of it made his heart shimmy with longing, but he pulled himself together and continued the walk to the steps, confused that the foyer chandelier wasn't lit. In fact, there was no light in the foyer at all. He walked to the light switch, not wanting to navigate stairs in the dark. When he flipped it, he got a quick glimpse of a crowd of people before they yelled, "Surprise!"

He froze. His grandmother had planned a surprise party?

If that didn't say she was regaining her spunk, he didn't know what did.

He walked down the stairs happy. He might not like a fuss being made over him, but it was what the fuss represented that filled him with joy.

His grandmother had planned a party.

She stood at the bottom of the stairs and, when he reached her, he kissed her cheek. "Thank you!" He looked beyond her to the crowd and said, "Thank you all."

He scanned the crowd again.

Then again.

Looking for Riley.

He wasn't sure if it was his grandmother's insistence that Riley loved him that made him believe GiGi might have invited her or wishful thinking, but his heart sank when he didn't see her.

He put on a brave face, laughed and chatted with his guests, but his gaze constantly roamed to the front door.

It never opened until the guests began to leave. Then he became jovial again. He slapped the backs of old friends and business acquaintances. Shook hands. Thanked everyone for gifts.

And then found himself very alone in the foyer when the last guest had gone.

"You really thought she'd come, didn't you?"

He peered over at his dad. His powers of observation were what made him such a good businessman, but right now Antonio wished he hadn't said anything.

"Drink?"

Antonio cleared his throat. "Bourbon."

"Ah. The drink of men with broken hearts."

"I thought that was wine."

Enzo laughed and led the way into the den. "Wine is good for everything."

Antonio followed him, though he wished he'd simply refused the drink and gone upstairs to his room. He was tired from pretending to be happy.

His father handed him a glass of bourbon. "You think she's as sad as you right now?"

Once again, he went back to pretending. "I have no idea."

"Oh, son. You forget how much alike we are. I know exactly what you're thinking. And I know you are thinking about her. About love."

Antonio stared at him. "Really? Because the last time I looked you haven't been in love since Mom."

Enzo laughed and got comfortable on the sofa.

"I was in love once." He peeked over at Antonio. "Before your mom."

Eager to hear that tale and forget about Riley, Antonio sat on a leather chair across from the sofa. "Really?"

"She was something."

"So why isn't she my mother?"

Enzo snorted. "Because I let her get away."

"Let her?"

"She wanted to study in Paris, and I told her I thought that was great, but I wouldn't go with her. I thought a visit or two would suffice and when her studies were over, she'd return home to me."

"But?"

"But she broke it off. Saw my not going with her as me not supporting her. I stubbornly stood my ground and she met someone else."

Not knowing what to say to that, Antonio just looked at his dad, waiting for details.

"You know that Riley's going to find someone else, right?"

Not wanting to think about that, he shifted on his seat and went back to pretending again. "Probably."

"Yeah. She's too pretty to stay single for long. Especially now that her business is established. I could read between the lines of her story. She threw herself into that company and now she's got something real."

"It's a solid company."

"And now that she knows that, I think she's realizing she can relax." He chuckled. "Dating you... coming to Italy every other week...was proof she trusts her staff enough that she can scale back. You know...go after what she wants."

"I wish her well."

"Oh, Antonio. You do not. You wish she was still here. And I'm not quite sure that she isn't."

"Because I can't give her what she wants."

His dad sat forward. "Really? And what is that?"

He knew better than to say, "Love." His dad would see right through that. A man didn't mope and pine for a woman he didn't love.

His breath stalled as that realization tried to take root. And he wouldn't let it. Watching his wife's love for him die and enduring the loss of his love for her were heartbreaking proof that love was temporary. He'd vowed he'd never risk that kind of pain again. He intended to keep that vow.

And his father should know that. "I can't give her a commitment."

Enzo frowned. "You lost me."

"Really? You must be forgetting Sylvia."

"Ack." He batted a hand. "She's your past. Riley could be your future."

"No, Dad. I'm not going down that road again and before you try to argue with me...clean up your own house. You did the same thing after Mom left."

He snorted. "So, because I made a big mistake, you're going to make the same mistake?"

"It wasn't a mistake. You protected yourself."

"I didn't protect myself. I hid. Then I never fell in love. There's a big difference between what happened with me and what's happening with you. *You're* wrong."

Tired, and only wanting to get to bed, Antonio rose. "Good night, Dad."

"Good night, Antonio. But just remember that Riley isn't Sylvia. Sylvia was like a butterfly. Beautiful. Fun. The kind of woman you like to make happy. Riley is the woman who makes *you* happy. The kind of woman you make a life with. She doesn't want your money. She has her own. The only reason she was with you was because she wanted to be." Enzo rose and headed back to the bar. "That's the difference. That's why you escape from one and keep the other."

The idea inched its way into his brain. He pictured himself with Riley for the rest of his life and there was no fear. Then he saw them having children and it felt as if an entire world, a world of possibilities, opened up to him. The firm foundation on which he believed he stood shifted and changed.

He wanted that.

All of it.

Not to please her but to have a new, happy life with her.

He didn't have to work to make her happy. They made each other happy.

He loved her.

He loved her...

And he had hurt the woman who made him believe in love again.

CHAPTER FIFTEEN

RILEY SAT IN the middle of the outdoor eating area of her favorite restaurant, just a smidge annoyed with Jake for keeping her at lunch for two hours. His where-is-my-life-going? crisis surprised her. She'd thought he was happy as the videographer for their proposals, but he seemed to want more.

At least that's what she thought this rambling conversation was about.

She could have guided him if he'd had a clearer understanding of what "more" was for him. But no. He had no idea what he wanted. So, she'd spent an hour detailing every job in her company and offering him the chance to train for different things. But he'd looked at his watch, then rolled into the possibility that he'd like to start his own company.

She'd listened to him prattle as long as she could before she'd motioned for the waiter to bring the check. She'd paid it, and they'd left the restaurant. Then, for a guy who'd been so gabby during lunch, he'd stopped talking. He'd sat beside her in the cab, playing a drum solo on the back of the passenger's seat in front of him, occasionally looking at his watch.

She could have swatted him. Instead, she started mentally running through that afternoon's work. Oddly, her schedule was clear. No proposals that afternoon. Nothing on the books to organize. She'd thought she had a prospective groom to talk to, but no. Somehow her schedule had magically cleared. She had no appointments or meetings. Otherwise, she could have gotten out of her conversation with Jake a lot sooner.

With nothing else to do, it was probably time to take a look at her notes from Italy and figure out how to beef up the rudimentary presentation she'd created for grooms who might want to propose while on vacation.

Or not. Up to now, she hadn't been able to look at her notes. Everything reminded her of Antonio and her broken heart. She wasn't sure today would be any different.

She couldn't believe she'd not only fallen in love, but she'd fallen in love with the worst possible person. She'd gone into her relationship with Antonio believing it would be an affair—and it had been a great affair until she'd connected with Italy as if she had been born to live there and saw another side of Antonio. The normal side: Not the billionaire playboy, but the man who loved the land and his family. The man who had so much to give but didn't see it.

The elevator door opened onto her floor. She plowed down the corridor and into the reception area of her office. Marietta jumped out of her seat. "You're back."

She grabbed the mail from Marietta's desk and began leafing through it. "Yes. Finally." She glanced behind her at Jake and winced. "Sorry. I know we didn't finish our conversation but maybe we can try again next week."

He gave her a sheepish look. "That's okay. I'll just keep thinking about my options here."

"Good. Because we can always hire another videographer, but you're beginning to understand the anatomy of a proposal now. You'd be great as someone who talked to clients and helped them decide what they want."

He grimaced, then sucked in a breath and smiled. "Sure. That sounds great."

He looked at Marietta as if seeking help.

Marietta glanced at her watch. "You know what, Riley? There is something you and I need to do this afternoon. Central Park is making some changes to Summerhouse at the Dene."

The place where Antonio had fake proposed to her and where they'd had their first kiss? Her stomach fell, but not wanting to give away her real feelings she happily said, "Really?"

"I think you and I need to go down there and check it out."

Her heart stuttered at even the possibility of

going back to the place where Antonio fake proposed to her. "We can't just call?"

"What if they're changing something major? We need to see it. We have four proposals there before Christmas."

"Wouldn't someone have called us if it wasn't available?"

Spreading her hands, Marietta shrugged. "Would they?"

Riley just looked at her. But she also realized she couldn't avoid that place for the rest of her life. Maybe it would be better to go back when she had nothing specific on the agenda, just wanted to see what changes they were making. She could go there, absorb all the memories, force herself to feel everything, then get herself on the real road to recovery.

She would love to feel better. She was tired of missing him, tired of wondering about what could have been.

Maybe what she needed was to see the place torn up, no flowers, no mandolins—just like her heart.

It really could be the first step to healing.

Marietta caught her arm and encouraged her out of the office. "Let's just go check it out. It won't take more than twenty minutes to get there and then we'll know for sure."

"Yes," she agreed as Marietta pushed her out the door. "After this we'll know better."

She liked the sound of that.

They caught a cab to Central Park. Riley paid the cab driver and followed Marietta into the park. The whole place had the oddest feel to it though. She decided that was because the world was caught between fall and winter. The early November air was cooling. Leaves had changed color and were drifting off trees. Everybody was preparing for Thanksgiving. People were living normal, everyday lives.

Exactly what she wanted.

Now she just needed to see Dene Summerhouse getting an overhaul and it would be the symbol of her getting on with her life.

Marietta said, "This way."

"Really? I thought it was that way."

Marietta smiled. "You can get to it a lot of ways."

"Okay."

As they walked up the path, voices floated to them. Probably subcontractors.

Laughter unexpectedly filled the air.

Which began to feel different again. She swore the whole place reeked of the anticipation of a proposal. Her favorite feeling in the world. And she probably felt it because she'd done more than a few events here.

The voices hushed.

They walked a few more feet and she could clearly see Dene Summerhouse. "There are no contractors here," she said, confused.

"Just keep going."

They walked up to the gazebo space and Marietta gave her a nudge. "We can't see much from back here, why don't you go check out the inside, see if you can tell what they're doing."

She frowned, wondering why Marietta wasn't coming with her. But it didn't matter. The place looked fine. Whatever Marietta had heard was wrong.

She walked into the gazebo and three violinists appeared out of nowhere. They began to play something soft and romantic.

She turned, confused, and ready to go back the way she had come, but she saw Antonio. And Jake, filming everything.

Her heart stumbled as Antonio climbed the steps. No one would ever be as handsome to her as he was. The love she felt for him filled her heart, but she also remembered that he didn't want what she wanted.

She opened her mouth to say, "What are you doing here?" But she only got out the "What—"

Antonio got down on one knee, pulled a ring box from his pocket, and said, "I love you. Will you marry me?"

Her heart pounded in her chest. The weirdest sense of déjà vu filled her. She wanted to say yes, as she had in the fake proposal, but she knew this wasn't what he wanted.

She leaned down and whispered. "What are you doing?"

"Asking you to marry me."

"You don't believe in love. You never want to marry again."

He rose, slid his arms around her and pulled her close enough that he could whisper in her ear. "I changed my mind. When you left, I looked around and realized the whole world was dimmer. Duller. I was lonely without you. Nothing had meaning. And that's when I saw it."

She pulled back so she could look into his eyes. "Saw what?"

"What you knew about love and connection and partners."

She studied his eyes which had darkened with sincerity.

"Love—getting married—isn't about sex and romance—though that part is fun—it's about believing."

"Believing?"

"Life is common unless you have someone or something you believe in. You make my life richer. You make me believe in possibilities again. You have shown me that I do have a future."

"Oh."

He bumped his forehead against hers. "So will you marry me?"

Her lips trembled but her heart filled. "Yes."

He pulled the ring out of his pocket. "Nothing starts until the ring is on your finger."

She laughed. "It is usually the cue."

He slid the ring on her finger and tears filled her eyes. "It's a different ring."

"The other one was for a fake proposal. This one is very real."

She nodded. "And it fits."

Then he kissed her. Having his lips on hers was like coming home. She could picture them raising their kids on his family's villa and coming to Manhattan for holidays and Christmas with her mom. She could see them growing old, watching their children take over the vineyards and the companies that had been built by Carlos, GiGi and Enzo.

But most of all, she could see their love, their commitment, enduring.

He broke the kiss, and the sound of the alleluia chorus filled the area. Thirty singing judges danced their way onto Dene Summerhouse and made a circle around them. Marietta and Jake stood off to the side applauding.

Her eyes filled with tears again. "I'm not a judge."

"No. But these judges clued me in that you were a proposal planner and that's why I approached you. I thought it fitting that they should oversee our real proposal."

She laughed. "Maybe this one will hold up in court."

"This one will hold up forever."

She brushed a light kiss across his lips. "That's exactly what I was thinking."

He turned to look behind him. "Jake, is this all on video?"

He waved his small camera. "Got it."

She realized then that Jake had stalled her at lunch so Marietta could throw all this together and she laughed. "Do you really think your GiGi's going to believe this?"

"Yes and no."

"Yes and no." She frowned. "I seem to remember somebody dissing me for not being able to make up my mind."

He pointed to the right, and she saw GiGi, Enzo and her mom standing together, clapping. The first thing she noticed was the bandana on GiGi's head.

"She started her chemo."

"Yes. I wasn't sure she should come but she insisted. We chartered a jet and came with a nurse. So she could see it all."

Riley laughed. "Seeing is believing?"

"I think the strength of her belief might depend on us getting married."

She stood on her tiptoes to kiss him. "The sooner we get married, the sooner I move into the villa."

"That," he said, "will seal the deal."

She loved the sound of that, loved that her life

had fallen into place. But most of all she loved that he felt the same way about her that she felt about him.

EPILOGUE

ANTONIO STOOD AT the bottom of the exam table, glancing around at all the "things" in the room where Riley would have an ultrasound to determine the sex of their first child. They were in Manhattan. The pregnancy had been a surprise, and she hadn't found a gynecologist in Italy yet. But they'd figure it out. Eventually. Not that he was nervous.

Much calmer than he was, Riley lounged on the piece of furniture that looked more like a chair than a table.

"Relax."

He faced Riley. "I'm fine."

"You're nervous."

He thought about that for a second. His case of jitters was not for himself but for her. He couldn't imagine being pregnant, let alone going through childbirth. Women were braver than any warrior for the challenges of bearing a child.

"I'm not nervous."

"Maybe you should be. A baby is going to change our lives."

He walked over and took her hand. "For the better."

She smiled. "I think so." Then she frowned. "But he or she comes with a lot of noise."

"GiGi will love that."

"We've taken her very quiet, sedate life and turned it upside down already."

"So having a child can't be that much more disruptive."

Her eyebrows raised as if she were about to argue, but the doctor walked in. "Are we ready?"

They both said, "Yes."

He washed his hands, then strolled over, pulling on his rubber gloves before he grabbed the wand. After a few seconds of prep work, he ran the wand over her stomach. Antonio expected him to say *It's a boy!* or *It's a girl!*

Instead, he frowned. "Well, Riley…" He glanced over at Antonio. "Antonio. It looks like you've got a twofer."

Antonio said, "Twofer?"

"Two for the price of one."

His eyes narrowed. "Two what for the price of one what?"

Riley gasped and squeezed his hand. "Oh, my God! Twins?"

The doctor grinned. "Twins."

Riley laid back and laughed. "Wow."

Antonio saw the whole situation through her eyes. She'd been an only child, didn't know her father's family, felt like an outcast. Then she heard the doctor say they were having twins, and her laughter came naturally, easily.

The man who didn't believe he'd ever have a family was about to become the father of twins.

She caught his hand. "It's great, isn't it? What we want?"

"It's exactly what we want." He squeezed her fingers. "GiGi's going to be over the moon."

He could tell from the expression in her eyes that she'd pictured it. "Yes. She is. So are my mom and your dad."

"Our family."

He squeezed her fingers again. "Our family." And a great adventure. He'd never thought of having kids. Never thought of marrying again. Now, it felt like the whole world had opened up to him.

So many possibilities. So much love.

* * * * *

Look out for the next story in
The Bridal Party trilogy

Mother of the Bride's Second Chance

And if you enjoyed this story,
check out these other great reads from
Susan Meier

Fling with the Reclusive Billionaire
Claiming His Convenient Princess
Off-Limits to the Rebel Prince

All available now!

HARLEQUIN
Reader Service

Enjoyed your book?

Try the perfect subscription for Romance readers and get more great books like this delivered right to your door.

See why over 10+ million readers have tried Harlequin Reader Service.

Start with a Free Welcome Collection with free books and a gift—valued over $20.

Choose any series in print or ebook. See website for details and order today:

TryReaderService.com/subscriptions